A GRAVE SITUATION

LIBBY HOWARD

CHAPTER 1

"I'll be there at seven," I promised Matt as I handed him a beer. He'd joined us for our Friday happy hour on the porch this week. Honestly I was surprised to see him. The charity golf tournament was tomorrow morning, and I assumed he had a million things to do. But Matt Poffenberger was one of the most energetic and organized men I'd ever met. He could juggle six events like this with a smile on his face, and they'd all go off without a hitch. I, on the other hand, was a frazzled mess and all I'd done was coordinate some hole sponsors and solicit baskets for the silent auction. My work should have been done, but Matt had just asked me to come drive one of the golf carts around that sold beer and wine as well as non-alcoholic beverages to the golfers at the tourney tomorrow. Which was probably one of the reasons he was here on my porch drinking a beer and not off making last minute calls or picking up signs or something.

"You've been a huge help, Kay." The man's smile was charming. "I owe you lunch for this."

He didn't owe me anything for this, but Matt always

found an excuse to treat me to coffee or lunch as a non-dating, platonic way of seeing me outside of the fundraisers I was helping him with. Between those not-dates, his occasional porch happy hour attendance, and the monthly lunches at the nursing home with him and his father, I saw Matt socially two or three times a month—much to Daisy's delight.

I didn't mind. He was my age, long divorced, fit and attractive. Okay, more than attractive. And he made no secret of the fact he'd be happy to move our not-dates into the actual date category if I wished. He was a good guy, a friend, and a lot of fun to be with, but I wasn't ready for that. I wasn't sure I'd ever be ready for that. So not-dates it was.

Ironic how I was urging my best friend to give the excruciatingly slow-burn romance she had with J.T. Pierson every chance to flourish and bloom, while I was definitely putting Matt into what Madison would have called the "friend-zone." Of course, Daisy wasn't newly widowed like I was.

Newly. It had been seven months since Eli had passed away. There were times that still felt raw and painful, and times when I felt the healing balm of time. It was the latter times I felt the guiltiest. Seven months and I was already beginning to heal? It seemed disrespectful, even though I knew Eli wouldn't have wanted me to mourn forever.

Although seven months was hardly forever. Heck, if I'd been a widow two hundred years ago, I would probably still have been wearing black clothing and not attending balls.

"I'm ready to win that trophy tomorrow, Matt." Judge Beck dug a beer out of the ice chest and grinned up at the other man.

Matt snorted. "Good luck with that. Those realtor women win every year."

"As long as we beat Smith, Barnes, and Dorvinski's *Legal Eagles* team this year, I'll be happy," the judge replied.

Each team had come up with a catchy name, and Matt had printed up signs for their golf carts and for the photo ops. Judge Beck's team was comprised of him and three of his judge buddies. The kids had brainstormed with us one night over tacos and come up with the name of *Guilty On The Green*. It had been Henry's idea and I still chuckled at how clever it was.

Matt nodded over to where Olive was chatting with Suzette and Daisy. "Watch out for the *Balance Sheet Babes* this year, too. The pro over at Oak Valley says that woman has a solid drive of over two-hundred and a darned good putt."

I did a double-take. "Olive? I didn't even know she golfed."

"I've seen her out on the course," Judge Beck admitted. "I didn't realize she was on a team this year. Guess we better hope for third place then."

"More like fourth place," Matt teased. "I've seen your putting, Nate. Those *Legal Eagles* are going to crush you judges."

"If I'd stayed in private practice and been able to keep a lovely nine-to-five, I'd have a better putting game," the judge complained.

I laughed, because I knew full well that the Smith, Barnes, and Dorvinski lawyers didn't keep nine-to-five at all. But if Judge Beck wanted to use that as an excuse for his lousy putting, I wasn't going to call him out on it.

"New rule this year, Matt?" Judge Beck asked with a grin. "Women need to tee off the men's tee. It's only fair, you know."

Matt smirked. "They'd still beat you, Nate."

I left the two to their golf banter and headed over toward Daisy, Suzette, and Olive, curious about my newest friend's talents. CPA. Golfer. And a medium who could communicate with the dead. What next, professional scuba diver? Expert in Ancient Korean culture? Donkey whisperer?

The subject of my wild imaginations was sipping a glass of Merlot, her hair an edgy up-do of beaded braids. She'd come straight from work in a taupe pants suit with a gorgeous plum and forest green infinity scarf draped around her neck and a designer bag over her shoulder.

"I hear you're the Tiger Woods of Locust Point," I teased her.

"My love of golf began on the Enchanted Planet putt-putt course at the age of six," she informed me. "The rest is history."

"Well, be warned that Judge Beck is over there lobbying for you to use the men's tee," I told her, not at all guilty for ratting out my roommate.

She snorted. "I'd still beat him. The man putts like he's using a weed wacker."

The comment caught Suzette mid-drink, and she sputtered, laughing and coughing at the same time.

Olive patted her on the back. "Careful, girl. I've already got one funeral to attend this week. Don't need another."

"Oh, no," Daisy chimed in. "Was it a relative? A co-worker?"

"My uncle." Olive shook her head. "It's a blessing really. He's no longer suffering and is finally at rest. I have a lot of fond memories of Uncle Ford and Aunt Sarah growing up. He was only diagnosed six months ago, but had been ill before that. Glioblastoma multiforme, they called it. Malignant brain tumor."

"I'm so sorry," I told her. "When is the funeral? And where?"

"Well…." She looked down at her half-empty wine glass. "Are you gals ready for a story? Fill this up, and I'll tell you about a family feud that you won't believe."

Daisy took off like a shot, bringing the entire bottle of Merlot over and keeping it at the ready after filling Olive's glass. The woman took a sip, then shot me a wry smile.

"Viewing is Wednesday, with the funeral and burial supposedly on Saturday. I know, I know, these things are supposed to happen at the end of the week and on the week-end, so folks can be off work and travel in, but my family? Well, we've got drama. Lots of drama."

Daisy picked up the wine bottle and topped off all of our glasses. "What kind of drama?" she asked in hushed tones.

Olive stared mournfully down at her glass. "People die and it seems like the vultures are circling before the sun goes down. There's some sister of Uncle Ford's who thinks she should be getting the china and silver instead of his wife because it was their mother's. Then there's always someone who claims the deceased promised them this or that, or owed them money or something. It's crazy."

Suzette wrapped an arm around Olive's shoulder. "Oh, I know. When Gran left me the family farmhouse, some of my aunts and uncles went crazy. They thought they should have gotten it. Although they would have sold it, and I'm pretty sure the reason Gran left it to me was because she knew I'd want to keep the house, to treasure the memories of genera-tions who'd lived there before me."

"Well, in my case, there's two sides of my family who are at odds. It was never really a feud or anything until this past year, but it's been building." Olive took another sip and looked a bit embarrassed. "Aunt Sarah and her first cousin, DeLanie. They were close growing up, but ever since their grandparents died—my great-grandparents—they've been poking at each other over who should get what. Didn't help that DeLanie's father passed before Great-grandma, so Aunt Sarah's mother got most of the family heirlooms as their only surviving child."

I was never so glad that Eli and I had been only children, our parents and grandparents long gone. Yes, we had cousins here and there, but no close relatives to come out of the woodwork upon Eli's death to insist that some painting or diamond cufflinks should have gone to them rather than me.

Not that there'd been any valuable paintings or diamond cufflinks.

Olive shook her head. "Just when the heirloom stuff got worked out, things went up in flames over the gravesites."

Daisy, Suzette, and I all exchanged equally perplexed glances. "Gravesites?"

"Get ready for math. And drama," Olive declared. "My great-grandparents bought eight cemetery plots back when my grandparents were only children. Sadly, they had to bury a daughter young, then Great-grandpa passed, then Great-uncle Morty, DeLanie's father. You with me so far?"

We all nodded, keeping count on our fingers.

"That's seven gravesites taken once they laid all my great aunts and uncles and my great-grandma to rest. So, one grave plot left, and three grandchildren—DeLanie from Great-uncle Morty's line, my father, and Aunt Sarah from Grandma's line. Still with me?"

I held up seven fingers. "Yep."

"Now, DeLanie figured the plot belonged to her because her father was the eldest of Great-grandma's children. Aunt Sarah said it should be hers or my father's because our grandmother survived Uncle Morty and at the time of Great-grandma's death, their mother was the only living child."

"Got it," I told her.

"Now, my father flat out told them he didn't want none of that. He was being cremated and stuck under that workshop he spends so much time at. Aunt Sarah didn't agree."

Daisy tilted her head and frowned. "Didn't agree with your father being buried under the workshop?"

"No, Aunt Sarah didn't agree with the plot going to DeLanie."

I was still holding up my fingers, which greatly hindered my ability to drink my wine. "Why didn't your great-grandparents buy just seven plots? The two of them, plus the daughter that died young, plus two other children and their spouses is seven. Why eight?"

Olive shrugged. "Maybe they figured my aunt that died young wouldn't die and would marry? Maybe it was a buy-seven-get-one-free deal? I've got no idea, Kay. All I know is that one extra plot is going to drive us *all* to an early grave."

"Wait." Daisy wiggled seven fingers. "So your great-grandparents are gone and buried. Their children and spouses are gone and buried. There's one plot left. Taking this to its natural conclusion, I'm assuming your Aunt Sarah wants that for your Uncle Ford? And cousin DeLanie feels it's hers?"

"Worse." Olive grimaced and took a healthy swig of her wine. "Six months ago, DeLanie lost her son to an overdose. David was only thirty—the same age as me. It was a horrible tragedy. Everyone put their differences aside to support her, because there isn't much worse in the world than having to bury your child."

We all nodded in sympathy. Then it suddenly dawned on me what the drama was.

"DeLanie buried her son David in the plot," I guessed.

Olive nodded. "No one thought about it at all. We were all feeling terrible for DeLanie. Then after the funeral when we went to the interment at the cemetery, there's David being buried in the one last plot—the one Aunt Sarah considered to be hers."

I caught my breath in horror. "Was there a scene?"

"There was a whole lot of muttering at the grave-side service, then afterward when we were all eating chicken salad sandwiches at the church, Aunt Sarah and DeLanie got into it. Yelling. Screaming. Fingers pointed in each other's faces." Olive shook her head. "All over a stupid piece of land in a cemetery. They've never gotten along. My whole life I remember there being friction between the two of them. But this was downright shameful. I love my Aunt Sarah, but DeLanie had just lost a child, a thirty-year-old son. Some things you just gotta let go. Priorities, you know?"

We nodded. Daisy offered Olive more wine, which she waved away.

"But even if David hadn't been buried there, it was only one plot," Suzette commented. "Was your Aunt Sarah really going to bury her husband there and have herself interred elsewhere? It seems like this was the best use for it after all—a tragedy, an unexpected death."

"Oh, tell that to Aunt Sarah!" Olive let out a bitter laugh. "Uncle Ford was very ill when David died and had a terminal diagnosis the very next week. Aunt Sarah claimed that she wanted to use the plot for him, then have herself cremated and put in the same plot. Evidently there's room to do that."

Daisy frowned. "If there's room to do that, then why not have your Uncle Ford cremated and put at the foot of one of the other family graves, and her at the foot of another? Seems like that's the easy solution."

"It would be if you were anyone but Aunt Sarah. I've got no idea what goes on in that woman's head. Last I heard, she was insisting that DeLanie dig up David's remains and move him somewhere else so she could bury Uncle Ford in the plot. It's crazy."

I sucked in a breath. "Oh, Olive. I'm so sorry. What a nightmare for you to be dealing with the loss of an uncle and this family feud at the same time. Is there anything we can do to help?"

"Pray for us." Olive chuckled. "Pray for us and keep that wine coming."

We did keep the wine coming, and by the time everyone wrapped up and walked home, I was a bit tipsy. Daisy stayed to help me clean up from the happy hour, while Judge Beck went in to make dinner. It was just him and me until Sunday when Heather brought Madison and Henry back over for our week, so I was pretty sure dinner would consist of either hamburgers or one of the frozen pizzas stuffed in the freezer. I actually enjoyed these no-fuss evenings where casual dining was frequently followed by movies downstairs with a tub of ice cream.

"I'd invite you to stay for dinner, but I hear you have other plans," I teased Daisy. Her offer to help clean up wasn't unusual, but there was a certain nervousness about her this evening, and I knew why.

"Thirty minutes. I'm packed and ready, and even three glasses of wine hasn't loosened this knot in the pit of my stomach," she confessed as she wiped the table with far more vigor than necessary.

"It'll be fine," I assured her. "You've been going out for over a month now. You enjoy his company. You love boating. It's going to be a wonderful trip. Just relax."

J.T. had asked Daisy to accompany him on a fishing trip to the Keys, and, in an impulsive moment, she'd agreed. He'd gone all out. Fancy hotel. Deep sea fishing charter.

Separate bedrooms.

Daisy hadn't even needed to insist. In fact, she'd seemed a bit disappointed when she'd told me about it. They weren't even adjoining rooms, either. I bit back a smile at the thought, because I knew exactly where my boss was going with that. His feelings for Daisy were clearly deep. He'd been courting her with the sort of slow-and-steady ease of a man looking toward the long game. They'd kissed, but he'd waited for Daisy to make every move forward to take their friendship into a more romantic and physical direction. There was no way he'd have booked them a shared room, and an adjoining one was a few cocktails away from something he'd rather they both be fully sober to participate in.

He wanted Daisy to mean it. No "oh, it was the wine talking," or any uncertainty. And having the entire decision laid at her feet made my friend nervous.

"What if I decide to not stay in my room?" She fretted. "What if I have a great time, and the whole sun-and-boat-and-beach setting convinces me to cross that line, but then I regret it later? What if...."

I set down the empty wine bottle and took her by the shoulders. "J.T. is a *good* man. If you get carried away and decide later that you want to back things up and take more time, he'll be okay with that. As long as you're honest with him, and with yourself, about your feelings, he'll give you as much time as you need."

Tears glistened in my friend's eyes. "I don't want to screw this up, Kay. I've screwed up every relationship I've ever had. I'm an unmarried woman pushing sixty. I'm no good at this sort of thing."

"J.T. is an unmarried man of the same age," I told her. "You think he doesn't worry about screwing this up too? Why do you think he'd been taking things so slow and letting you make all the moves? Daisy, just have fun. Fish. Get some sun. Drink a frozen margarita with an umbrella in it. Dance until the sun comes up. Watch the sun rise over the ocean. And if you end up in bed with a good man who adores you, then enjoy yourself and don't overthink it."

Daisy rubbed her face. "You're right. It's just...scary. It's been a long time, you know? I probably just need to get laid."

"It's been a long time for all of us," I muttered, picking up the wine bottles again.

Daisy laughed. "Well, you need to get laid, too. And when I get back, I'm seriously sitting you down for a talk about your future."

"When you get back, I'd rather hear about your amazing vacation and how you're falling in love with J.T.," I told her. "Now get going. He's picking you up in another fifteen minutes. And don't be calling me unless you need bail money."

Daisy gave me a quick hug and skipped down the porch stairs. "I'd hardly be calling you for bail money when I'm on vacation with a bondsman."

I watched her go, then headed inside, a smile still on my face. Anxiousness aside, this was the happiest I'd seen Daisy in a long time. I hoped things worked out between her and J.T. I hoped she came back from this vacation head-over-heels in love. I wanted all that for my best friend, all that and more.

CHAPTER 2

"*I*'ll admit that it's intriguing from a legal standpoint, this thing about Olive's family feud over a gravesite," Judge Beck commented as we cleaned up after our hamburger-and-potato-chip-dinner—him washing and me drying. The dishwasher had been on the fritz, and with the kids over at Heather's house this week, it fell to the pair of us to clean the dishes. Let's just say there had been a lot of paper plates for the last few days.

"And it's intriguing from a golf standpoint as well," the judge added.

I whacked him with the dish towel. "Stop. The poor woman lost her uncle, and this family drama isn't making that loss any easier to deal with."

"I know, I know. Believe me, I'm sorry for her loss, and I truly feel for what she's going through. But a horrible part of me secretly hopes she's off her game tomorrow."

"Yes, that's pretty horrible," I scolded, taking a plate from the drying rack. "I know there's nothing we can do, but I'm curious about that legal standpoint you'd mentioned. If this came up before you as a judge, hypothetically of course, how would you rule?"

"First, I'd never see this because thankfully I'm a Circuit Court Judge and not a District Court one. This kind of civil suit is a nightmare. You couldn't pay me enough to rule on this."

"What if you had to, though? Or what if you were back in private practice and needed to think about precedent and all that other stuff?"

He sighed. "First thing would be to look at the great-grandparents' wills. Burial plots are part of the estate, and if the will didn't specify, then the records from the executor of the estate should have noted what the final distribution of assets was."

I blinked in surprise. "Huh. I hadn't thought of that."

"You probably didn't have to open an estate and go through probate when your husband died, because everything is considered marital property, and in the absence of a will to the contrary, all assets and debts automatically go to the spouse."

I paused, dried plate in my hand as I contemplated his statement. A lawyer had handled things when my father had passed, and I remembered one handling the estate when Eli's mother had died as well. Neither of us had been all that involved other than signing by the "x's." But then again, we'd both been only children with no family to fight over who got the silver and the loveseats.

Eli hadn't had a will. I'd recently been thinking about putting together one of my own, but I wasn't in any particular hurry to do so. If Eli and I had children, I probably would have just assumed they would have worked things out between them. Maybe I would have had a generic will stipulating they divide the estate equally between them. But what if there had been a coveted item, or something that didn't divide evenly?

As if summoned by the memory, I saw a shadow out of the corner of my eye, floating near the kitchen island. The ghost I was convinced was that of my late husband tended to appear in the evenings, a comforting presence that followed me from room to room and often remained near my bed as I slept. In the few months after his death, I'd seen his ghost during the day, but lately he only seemed to appear at night.

I dreaded the day he didn't appear at all. How would I feel to have him gone forever? The thought tightened my chest and brought a sting of tears to my eyes.

I cleared my throat, trying not to think about when that day might come.

"I'm assuming Olive's great-grandparents didn't have a will, or if they did, it was fairly vague," I told the judge as I put the plate in the cabinet. "Would the estate records have all the details, such as who got the grave plot?"

"They're supposed to. But from what I know about probate law and my having the occasional lunch with Judge Crawford, estate records sometimes only show the transfer of major items such as real estate, stocks, and cash. The rest ends up a line item as household goods with either a cash equivalency or a write-off as donated. And there's a lot that doesn't get reported. People don't like the government to know that they got a bunch of diamond jewelry from their mother, and they're worried they'll be taxed for those things, even though the bar for taxation on inheritance is so high that few estates reach that level."

I grimaced, thinking that I didn't have enough in my name to interest the IRS in my estate. The sale of the house would barely cover the mortgages at this point. There was a tiny life insurance policy I'd taken out when Eli had passed away to ensure there was enough money to bury me. Truly the only important thing was that the people I loved could get an item or two to cherish and hopefully remember me by.

"Well, I'm assuming there wasn't anything detailing who got what grave plot, or one of Olive's relatives would have been waving that in everyone's faces," I told Judge Beck. "Is there anything else that might hint at who should get what? Some sort of eldest-gets-the-most clause in the law?"

"No. They'd duke it out in court, and if neither side could present proof of the original owner's intent or proof of inheritance rights, then the judge would most likely assign a cash equivalence and basically toss a coin. One side gets the grave plot. The other pays the cash equivalence. And they both spend more on lawyers than what two dozen gravesites would have cost them."

"Seriously?" I picked up a handful of silverware and began drying it.

"Seriously."

"Toss a coin?"

He shot me a sideways glance. "Yeah, but don't tell anyone about that. Sometimes you just need to make a call and get everyone out of your courtroom. After hours of arguing and a convoluted presentation of exhibits without any one side doing more than spinning the same thing over and over, you just want it to end. When it's someone's life on the line, or their freedom, that's something you take seriously. But six hours of testimony on a family squabble over a grave plot? Where there's no definitive way to verify what the owner's intent was? Coin toss."

"Can't say I'm approving of this side of you, Judge Beck," I huffed.

"That's why I'm in Circuit Court and not in District Court. Let the other judges deal with this stuff in between people fighting their speeding tickets and red-light camera citations. There are juries in my court room. My job is to make sure the lawyers play by the rules and the juries do their jobs, not to make the call on which of six cousins gets their great-grandmother's turkey platter. Or the extra gravesite."

I understood, but I still wished there had been some sort of cut-and-dry legal ruling for this sort of thing. "Poor Olive."

"You know, she might want to check with the cemetery," Judge Beck added, shooting me a sympathetic glance. "Sometimes they keep records of that sort of thing."

"I'll say something, but I'm sure they've already checked." I couldn't imagine the cemetery would have had anything beyond the original purchase contract for the plots, and a record of who was buried where. Unless someone had presented them with a will or something from the estate, I doubt they would have noted who owned what plot beyond the original buyers.

When Eli had died, we hadn't made prior arrangements. I'd scraped together our savings and paid for the funeral, opting for a modest casket, a viewing, and purchasing a plot at the cemetery. I'd been so stricken with grief and guilt that I'd not done enough, not seen the signs of his stroke in enough time to get him help, that I'd poured nearly every last dime into his service and interment. Seven months later, I thought back on that with regret. Eli would have been furious with me for putting money into a casket and grave plot that could have gone to help with the mortgage and household expenses, but emotions seemed to take the wheel during those moments in our lives.

I made a mental note to not only get my will finalized, but to try to pre-pay as much of my funeral arrangements as possible. Cremation. Burial at the foot of Eli's grave. An addition on his headstone. Maybe a few thousand for a memorial service. With enough planning on my part, whoever got saddled with handling these things should have as little work and expense as possible.

"Why don't they just buy more plots?" Judge Beck asked, rinsing the final dish and putting it in the drainer.

"Because when someone buys a block of burial plots seventy or eighty years ago, the ones surrounding that group get sold. Olive's family could buy more plots, but they'd be off in a different section of the cemetery from the rest of the family. Her father doesn't seem to care, and I don't think Olive cares either, but clearly her aunt and this cousin want to be buried with their parents, grandparents, and siblings, and not halfway across the cemetery."

"Halfway across the cemetery." The judge shook his head. "You make it sound like their kids would need to drive to a different state to visit their graves. That's what? A hundred yards at most?"

"I guess it's the same thing as with family heirlooms and stuff," I told him. "Suzette inherited her family home and that means a lot to her with all the memories and such. I can see where being buried alongside generations of family would be important. It kind of harkens back to the old family grave-yards of old, you know?"

"Plus, I'm sure there's a strong sense of 'these are mine and I shouldn't have to pay for additional plots' as well." Judge Beck dried his hands and leaned against the counter. "But you're right. There's usually more to these issues than money. I'll bet there's an old issue between the two sides of the family adding to the disagreement. But I'm not a thera-pist, so I'm not going to weigh in on that one."

"All I know is Olive's uncle is supposed to be buried next Saturday, and this fight over a grave plot is a very unwelcome distraction at a time when people should be remembering a loved one and trying to gain closure about his illness and death."

"You're right. And I'm sorry I made light of it with my insensitive golf-game comment." The judge pushed away from the counter and took a few steps closer. "I'm sure this hits a raw nerve with you, Kay, having just lost your husband this year."

I nodded, thinking that maybe a lot of my sympathy for Olive's Aunt Sarah was because she was in the same position I'd been this spring—recently widowed and trying to both grieve and pick up the pieces of her life. I would have thought a family feud over a grave plot would be the last thing I'd want to stir up at this time, but who knows? Maybe part of her solace over losing her husband was wanting him to be in the family section of the cemetery. And maybe his loss uncovered other wounds that had never really healed.

I eyed Judge Beck. "So, early night for you? You've got a big day tomorrow. You'll want to be well rested. Unless you're thinking you should stay up and maybe practice your putting," I teased.

"Oh, not you too!" He pretended to look hurt. "One bad game, and suddenly everyone thinks I can't putt. If I didn't know better, I'd think you and Matt were trying to give me a complex, to psych me out. If I'm cursed, I'm blaming it on the two of you."

I held up my hands. "Hey, I've never seen you play. Just repeating what I heard on the porch tonight."

He smiled and followed me out of the kitchen toward the parlor. "Speaking of which, it's starting to get chilly out in the evenings. When do you usually call it quits on the happy hour ritual for the season?"

I gathered up my knitting and plopped down in a chair while Judge Beck took the couch.

"Honestly, I don't know. After Eli's accident, we didn't entertain, so this year's porch happy hour is a new thing for me. It *is* getting kind of chilly, though. You're right."

He sprawled back against the couch cushions, his brow furrowed in thought. "Maybe we could get one of those outdoor propane heater things for the porch. The tall ones that look like lamp posts, although I guess they couldn't be too tall or they'd set the porch roof on fire."

I grimaced at the thought of my porch in flames. "Do you think one of those would put out enough heat? I'm envisioning all of us huddled around it, shivering and trying to drink wine with mittens on."

"I could look into it," he mused. "I think they would suffice. Maybe get two of them?"

"I'm not sure it would be worth it. If it's thirty degrees out, I can't imagine people wanting to hang out for hours on a porch even with a heater. Besides..." I wrinkled my nose. "I think I'd rather spend the money on getting the dishwasher fixed."

"Can I admit that I'm finding the manual dish cleaning to be a bit fun?"

I laughed. "Well, I doubt Madison and Henry are finding it fun."

"No, Madison and Henry are most definitely not finding it fun. I think we're about to encounter a union drive and possibly a labor strike if we don't get it fixed soon. When *are* the parts supposed to be in, anyway?"

I squirmed, bending my head to seem as if I was focusing on my knitting. There were no hard-to-get parts on order. The repair man had charged me sixty dollars for the service call, then informed me that I needed to replace the appliance, that the cost of the parts and labor to install them was almost as much as a new unit, and there were issues with the current dishwasher that made it unwise to throw more money into it.

I'd lied, hoping to drag the mythical parts ordering process out for a few weeks until I could manage to pull the money together to get a new one. Six hundred dollars. Plus, the plumber's fee to install it. We were going on two weeks without a dishwasher and I didn't even have half that saved up.

"It's an old unit," I told Judge Beck. "They're having a hard time finding a place that has the parts."

The judge shook his head. "Seems like no one plans on fixing anything beyond five years anymore. Too bad that guy across the street passed away, because I'm sure he probably had five of the exact same dishwasher in his garage and backyard that you could have cannibalized for parts."

Mr. Peter had been a hoarder, but he'd also been an appliance repair technician before his retirement, and a lot of the junk in and around his house were projects he'd always intended to get to but never found the time. He'd probably had a few duplicates of my dishwasher somewhere over there, but in the last five months, his nephew had made great strides toward cleaning all the junk from the house. Originally, he'd begun with the house itself, finally resorting to a huge dumpster that sat in the driveway with an increasing number of boxes, papers, and broken items in it. He'd told me a few months ago that he was worried about winter and being unable to tackle the stuff in the yard if he waited, so that became his priority.

One day two Junk Jocks trucks pulled up in front of the house, and a host of strapping young men began loading them up with mowers, appliances, and broken lawn furniture. Will Lars had been so thrilled to see the clean-up efforts that he'd come over to lend a hand. By the end of September, the only sign of Harry Peter's hoarding was a bedraggled overgrown lawn dotted with geometric spots of mud and browned grass. It looked horrible, but compared to how the yard had looked for the last twenty years, it was an improvement.

But even if the dishwashers *had* still been there, I wouldn't have asked Mr. Peter's nephew for salvage parts. There was no sense in trying to resurrect my most definitely deceased dishwasher.

"Kay?" Judge Beck's voice was soft and tentative. "I don't mind waiting for the repair, truly I don't. It makes no difference to me whether I'm hand-washing coffee cups or not, and honestly, it's good for the kids to do a little bit of chore work. I really don't mind, but if it's bothering you, I'd be happy to buy a new dishwasher."

I shook my head and gave him a quick smile. "Let's see if the parts arrive in the next two weeks. If they don't, then I'll think about maybe buying a new one."

He was silent for a moment. "I don't want to insult you. I could lend you the money if you need, though. Put it on my credit card, and you could pay me back next month. It really would be no bother. I just don't want you worrying over this."

"Oh, I'm not worrying," I lied. "I hate to throw away a perfectly good major appliance if they can fix it, though. It just seems like such a waste. If the parts aren't here in two weeks, I'll go ahead and get a new one."

Two weeks. I wasn't sure I could get the money together in two weeks, and in spite of Judge Beck's very genuine offer, I didn't want to start down the road of borrowing money from him, or letting him pay for things like this. It was my house, my responsibility. He was the tenant here. He shouldn't have to front me the money for an appliance or loan me his credit card. I needed to be able to take care of these things myself. I needed to be more careful with my money, make sure I had adequate savings to cover things like this. Maybe if I stopped eating the occasional lunch out, cut back on groceries a bit, and....

There was nowhere else to cut back. I hadn't bought

clothing in years. Daisy had treated me to having my hair and nails done last month, but I had no intention on continuing that myself. I didn't have a gym membership, or anything else to cut out of my budget. I thought of the hot-tub repair I'd been able to pay off by selling that hideous vase, how a car repair last month had taken a huge bite out of my emergency fund. And now this dishwasher.

What if the roof started to leak? Or a pipe broke? It was October and I was starting to think about firing the furnace up for the coming colder weather. Oh, Lord, what if the furnace didn't start?

I tried to steady my breathing, noticing that I'd just knitted two rows of completely the wrong pattern on the scarf I was making for Suzette. As I started to unravel my stitches, I saw Judge Beck eying me over the edge of his book.

Two more weeks. One problem at a time.

And seriously, this really was one of those first world problems. Having to hand-wash dishes didn't constitute a crisis. If it had been me living here alone, or if Eli had still been alive, I wouldn't have bothered to replace the thing. I completely realized that this was more about my embarrassment over being unable to afford a new dishwasher, and particularly Judge Beck knowing I couldn't afford one.

Daisy already knew. But Judge Beck…I didn't want him to think me poor. I didn't want him thinking he had to jump in and bail me out every time something went wrong with the house. I didn't want our relationship sullied by the grime of lent money.

And because of that, I found myself in the position of having to come up with an additional four hundred dollars in the next two weeks.

CHAPTER 3

"*H*ave you tried that secondhand appliance store in Milford?" Suzette asked me as she expertly tooled the golf cart around a corner.

"Secondhand appliances?" The image of Mr. Peter's junk-filled yard came to mind. "I'm not sure I want to replace an old broken-down dishwasher with another old broken-down dishwasher and pay a few hundred dollars for the privilege."

Suzette pulled the golf cart up close to the third hole, and we watched the *Balance Sheet Babes* take their putts. Being in charge of one of three drink carts at the tourney was a complete blast. The hosting golf course was donating twenty percent of beverage sales to the Fill the Food Bank drive the tourney benefited. I wasn't sure that factored into the amount we were selling or this was normal behavior amongst golfers, but people were downing booze like the state had just reenacted prohibition.

Ten teams filled the eighteen-hole golf course. It was a best-ball scramble, whatever that meant. Scramble must have been something fun because the golfers were shouting and laughing, ribbing each other over a shot gone awry and racing all over the fairway in their golf carts like a bunch of Keystone Cops.

I'd quickly discovered there was also an ego thing that involved playing fast enough so that the team behind you wasn't waiting. Evidently allowing another group to "play through" in these tournaments was an embarrassment. And there was some cache in playing quick enough to rush the team ahead of you, to be able to stand at the tee, waiting, and making criticisms about their play.

I didn't care as long as they all had fun and we raised our goal for the food bank.

"Those appliances are used, but the people there fix them up before they sell them," Suzette told me. "Lots of people with rental places buy there. It's a good way to get a sturdy reliable appliance cheap if you don't mind that it doesn't have all the bells and whistles and might have a ding or two on the door. I bet you could get a pretty nice one for a few hundred dollars."

I thought about the embarrassment of replacing an old dishwasher with another old, albeit functional, one and winced. But it was a good fallback plan if someone didn't show up with a sack of money on my doorstep and I didn't have enough for a new appliance in two weeks.

"Can you text me the name of the place?" I asked Suzette. "I'll run by on Monday and check it out."

We didn't have time to discuss my appliance woes any longer, because the Balance Sheet Babes were done putting and were heading toward our beverage-laden golf cart as if they were coming out of the desert.

"I'll take a Coors Light, please," one woman told me, smoothing a gloved hand over her forehead.

"Better take two, Tricia," Olive told her. "After that sand trap? Seriously, you already worked off those calories."

"Stupid wedge." Tricia laughed, paying me for the two beers. "I need a better club."

"It's always the club's fault," one of the other women agreed, signaling that she'd like another Budweiser to replace the empty one in her hand. How she'd managed to putt while still carrying her beer was beyond me. These were clearly some talented ladies.

"Blame the club, the shoddy grounds keeping, the guy ahead of you who didn't replace a divot, a sudden wind…." Olive snickered. "Anything but the fact that you haven't been on a course or practice range in three months."

"You try juggling a new payables system at work and three new employees." Tricia laughed, taking a swig out of one of her bottles.

"It's not work, it's the internet dating," one of the other women teased. "All those men blowing up your phone, girl."

Tricia laughed. "Ninety percent of those men are internet scammers in some third-world country trying to get me to send them money for an 'emergency.' Please."

They all finished paying for their drinks, went back to their golf carts, and were off in a rush. I looked up the fairway and saw the next group already midway down.

"I'm glad Olive's enjoying herself," I told Suzette. "After what she told us last night about her uncle, I was worried."

"It's good for her to get out like this and not think about it," the other woman agreed. "There's really nothing she can do, and it's all so stressful. Hey, we're both going out for sushi later today. Want to join us?"

Suzette and Olive had met at one of my get-togethers and had fast become friends. Besties, as Madison would have called them. They were always off together checking out festivals, new restaurants, museums, and different bands. I loved hearing about their weekend plans and tried to go along when I was invited. These two were a total hoot and so much fun to hang out with.

But as inexpensive as sushi was, I was on a budget. And unagi definitely wasn't in that budget.

"Maybe next time," I told Suzette, thinking that perhaps I should swallow my pride and think about buying one of those no-frills cheap, secondhand appliances. Maybe then I could afford to go get sushi with my friends.

We drove on to the next team, carefully checking before driving across the fairway of the fifth hole to make sure no one beaned us with a ball. By noon we had to swing back to the clubhouse to restock our more popular beers. The sun was really beating down on us today, and I was sweaty in spite of the cool October weather, so I decided to splurge and get a beer for myself.

Matt waved away my money. "I appreciate you helping out today, Kay. Least I can do is buy you a beer. Actually, how about we grab some pizza tomorrow night. My treat for all your hard work getting sponsors for the tourney."

I hesitated.

"We can go over the numbers for the food bank," he quickly added. "And discuss which companies to hit up early for next year's hole sponsorships."

Matt had quickly learned to phrase his "non-dates" in a way that made them sound...well, made them sound like a non-date. Sometimes he emphasized the two-friends-getting-together angle, but mostly he used his charity work as the excuse. It was never anywhere too fancy or intimate, and he always insisted on paying. Although we did often discuss the charity work, that was usually over within the first half hour, and the rest was devoted to personal conversation.

I liked Matt. I liked doing these charity things with him. It gave me a sense of purpose, made me feel like I was giving back to the community. It was also nice to know there was an attractive man who thought I was worth spending time with. But beyond that...let's just say I was careful not to encourage Matt to take these non-dates in a different direction.

Much to Daisy's chagrin.

I politely explained I had other plans, promising to do lunch in a week or so, then Suzette and I took off, zooming around for hours selling beverages to thirsty golfers. When the last team was in with their scorecards, Suzette and I parked the golf cart, settled up with the beverage manager, and went into the clubhouse to join the festivities.

Everyone had a beer or wine in hand, making me a bit worried about who was driving all these tipsy golfers home. The alcohol seemed to be doing the trick, though, because the silent auction was closing down and from the jubilant expression on Matt's face, it seemed bidding had been higher than normal.

I grabbed a plate of food and a sweet tea, then headed through the crowd, searching for someone I knew.

"Mrs. Carrera! Kay! Hey there!"

I turned at the greeting and blinked, not recognizing the deputy for a moment without his uniform.

"Miles! Goodness, I didn't know you golfed."

His face turned red. "I don't. And if you saw our score sheet, you'd realize that. The county team needed a sub and I drew the short straw."

I patted his shoulder. "It's all for charity, Miles. No one is going to be ribbing you about your handicap."

"Yeah, well, you don't know the guys at work," he muttered. "I kept hoping I'd get an urgent phone call, but just my luck that crime decided to take a vacation today."

"Well, just for being a good sport, swing by the office Monday. I'll bring pastries. What's your favorite?"

His face brightened at the prospect. It might be a stereo-type, but I got the feeling the way to Miles's heart was truly through his stomach. Which made me wonder why he was still single. He was a nice-looking guy. He was sweet as could be. And he was a cop.

But I wasn't a matchmaker, in spite of my tentative success at encouraging J.T. and Daisy.

"The double chocolate muffins were my favorite," he confessed with a shy smile. "But those espresso chip scones sure were good, too."

I nodded, my mind still thinking over who I could pair this detective with. "How old are you, Miles?"

He blinked. "Old enough that it's okay if you put some rum in those double chocolate muffins, Mrs.—I mean Kay."

I grinned. "Humor me. How old are you?"

"Twenty-six," he told me. "Is that a problem? Do you only make pastries for the over thirty crowd?"

"Silly. Come by Monday morning, and I'll get you all muffined up."

I walked away, realizing that probably didn't sound right. Oh, well. I was sure Miles didn't think someone my age was hitting on him. Instead, my brain was trying to think of who I could possibly set him up with. I didn't know a lot of twenty-something women. Violet Smith? Hmm.

Judge Beck was over in the corner with the other members of his team. I took a few steps that way, only to hesitate. They all looked so intimidating standing there, drinks in hand as they discussed…whatever. Judge Beck was the youngest among them. The other three were all my age and older by what I could tell. That shouldn't have bothered me. I didn't normally have any problem walking up to anyone and having a conversation. I wasn't sure why suddenly these men seemed unapproachable. I just felt that if

I went over there, I'd seem like some silly schoolgirl interrupting her betters.

So instead I detoured over to where Olive and her team were laughing over the contents of one of the silent auction baskets they'd won. Suzette had already made her way there and was chatting with one of the other women. I saw Olive take her phone out of her pocket, look at the screen, then move away from the others with a frown as she answered it.

Oh, no. I hoped the good day she'd had wasn't about to come to an end. Sharing a concerned glance with Suzette, I turned to see what was in the basket.

Spices. Really fancy spices. And really fancy coffee. And a cookbook full of fancy recipes. "See something you like?" one of the ladies asked me. "We're sharing it. Pick out a spice. Or take this recipe book."

I picked it up and paged through it, figuring that Madison might like to try a dish or two from it. Or I might. Kentucky short ribs looked pretty darned good.

"I'm sorry, but I have to leave." Olive's voice was strained, and I turned to see her clutching her phone, her lips in a tight line.

"Everything okay?" I whispered.

She shook her head.

"Your uncle?" Suzette asked, putting a hand on the other woman's shoulder. "Can I help? What can I do?"

Olive sighed. "You know, I hate to ask the two of you to do this, but I really don't want to be alone right now. Can you both come with me to the cemetery? They're disinterring my cousin, David."

CHAPTER 4

*M*y eyes nearly fell out of my head.

"What?" Suzette exclaimed. "For your Uncle Ford? I can't believe your Aunt Sarah really went that far!"

"I know." Olive rubbed her forehead. "Evidently, she's paying for it, and the sick thing is for the cost of disinterring David's remains and burying him elsewhere, she could have bought half a dozen plots. But no, she's fixated on this one, and cousin DeLanie finally gave in. I feel so sorry for her."

Suzette hugged Olive. "Of course I'll come."

"I'm so sorry. I'll definitely come too," I told Olive, at a loss about what to say. It was so unfair that they had to go through all this, so unfair that her aunt just couldn't let the past stay in the past.

"The worst thing is Aunt Sarah wants me to be there. Now. They're digging him up now, and she can't face DeLanie, so she wants me to be there." Olive sniffed, her mouth twisting. "I almost said 'no.' I love Aunt Sarah. She was so good to me when I was a child, and I just can't reconcile this woman with the one I grew up with. Maybe Uncle

Ford's death broke something in her, because this is just wrong. Asking a cousin to dig up her child.... It's wrong."

"Asking you to be there is wrong," Suzette shot back. "She's the one pushing this feud. You shouldn't have to be the buffer between her and DeLanie."

"I know. She wants me to be there...I don't know, I guess to witness it all or something. I'm going more to let DeLanie know that not everyone on our side of the family supports this madness. And maybe to let her know I'm sympathetic to what she's going through here. Whether that grave plot was hers or not doesn't matter in my mind. She'd buried her son there. It's only respectful to let him lie. Besides, she shouldn't be alone while they move David. And I'd feel a lot better if I had some friends with me."

I tracked down Matt and let him know that Suzette and I needed to leave early. Our work at the tourney was pretty much done anyway. I'd intended on staying and helping Matt with clean up and running the totals, but he had enough volunteers to assist him, so I didn't feel like I was skipping out on a commitment. Besides, if Olive needed me along for moral support, then I was going to be there.

Suzette went with Olive in her car, while I followed in my own. Windy Oaks wasn't the oldest cemetery in town, but it had been around for over a hundred years. Olive's great-grandparents had purchased their plots when it wasn't quite as large as it was now. Driving down the narrow maze of lanes, I passed by the turn to Eli's grave. I'd only been able to afford a small rectangle engraved marker, but a few rows down were a few huge monuments and tall rounded headstones.

Olive's family section looked pretty much like the rest of the cemetery. Neat rows of big rectangular markers were interspersed with the same flat rectangular stones I'd used for Eli's grave. Their marker announced this section held those in the Driver family, and I quickly went through Olive's family tree in my head, reconciling the Driver family name with Olive's last name of Johnson and her aunt and uncle's last name of Branch.

A large white canopy had been erected over the spot close to where we parked. It reminded me of the set up for the graveside service we'd held, the only difference being the small excavator parked at the end of the grave. A rough-hewn wooden box sat next to it all, to hold the dirt, I supposed. Off to the side was a small flatbed truck with a hoist attached.

Three men stood around the grave site, dressed in neat work overalls. A woman in her late twenties stood next to them. And all around them were ghosts.

The shadows made the whole cemetery seem murky and foggy. I hadn't remembered seeing all these ghosts when I'd buried Eli, or when I'd come to visit his grave. Yes, in the last seven months I'd seen the occasional shadowy spirit out of the corner of my eye while here, but nothing like this. It was as if an entire mob of ghosts had gathered to bear witness to the relocation of these remains.

The woman approached us. She was nicely dressed in a pantsuit with tasteful jewelry and subtle makeup. Her hair in a neat bun low on the back of her head, and she fiddled with a chain at her neck, tucking what looked to be a circular pendant in the collar of her crisp button-down shirt. She was carrying a clipboard and a pen in the other hand. I recognized her from when I'd organized Eli's interment, but couldn't remember her name.

"Are you the next of kin?" she asked Olive in a voice that was the perfect mix of calm efficiency and mild sympathy—flat but kind. Inoffensive, with just enough emotion to keep from sounding...well, unfeeling.

"No, I'm Olive Johnson, here to represent Sarah Branch. I'm her niece."

The woman nodded and tapped the clipboard. "I'm Melanie Swanson, cemetery manager here at Windy Oaks. I'll be calling your aunt later today about the arrangement for her husband. I'm so sorry for your loss, Mrs. Johnson."

Olive glanced over to the grave. "I'm sorry we're putting you through all this, Miss Swanson."

"Oh, please call me Melanie. And it's no trouble at all. We're always here to help families during their time of grief," the woman replied with a practiced graciousness. "That does occasionally include relocation of a loved one."

She was just as diplomatic as I'd remembered her. It made me wonder if she ever cut loose once she was out of the cemetery grounds. I tried to envision her angry and cursing up a storm at someone, or drunk and dancing around with a lampshade on her head, and failed.

"We do need to wait until Ms. Driver arrives as next of kin," Melanie said with an apologetic smile that managed to include all three of us. "I've put some chairs over to the side if you all would like to sit."

"How long…" Olive grimaced. "I'm sorry. I don't want to sound disrespectful, like I'm trying to rush this along or anything. I'm just wondering what to expect."

Melanie nodded. "Completely understandable. Generally during this time of year, it takes about forty-five minutes to an hour for us to open a grave in preparation for interment. As we're doing a relocation, some of the work will be done by hand as opposed to using the excavator. We will make every effort to be respectful and careful in our handling of, David, so expect around two hours."

Olive glanced out across the cemetery. "Is DeLanie having him immediately re-interred? Is there a service? I feel so horrible not knowing these things. I mean, she's my cousin."

"She's having him immediately interred, but planned a private service for Sunday. I do believe she is wanting to bless the new grave." The woman's gaze shifted toward an approaching car. "This must be Ms. Driver. If you'll excuse me?"

Without waiting for a response, she was off, clipboard in hand, that efficient yet mildly sympathetic expression firmly in place.

"If you all want to head out, I completely understand," Olive told Suzette and me. "I hate the thought of you all sitting here for two hours. It's going to be so awkward."

"We're not going anywhere until this is over," Suzette insisted. "And when it's done, you're coming back to my place for a few big glasses of wine and pizza delivery. You can spend the night so you don't have to worry about driving."

"I'm staying," I told her as we went over and sat in the chairs. "We're here for you. And hopefully once today is over, you'll be able to focus on grieving for your uncle and putting all this family bitterness behind you."

Melanie came toward us, a tall woman by her side. DeLanie Driver was matronly in build and wore a somber knit dress that matched the color of her short silver-gray hair. Olive rose as she approached, hugging her and nearly crushing the box of tissues the other woman carried.

"I'm so sorry, DeLanie. I hate that this is happening."

The older woman smiled, her eyes swimming in tears as she patted Olive on the arm. "I know, I know. Sarah and I have always had our differences, but I've never had any issues with your father or your family, Olive. And David always loved you. Remember when you were both little and you'd swing out in the backyard together?"

Olive nodded, helping herself to a tissue from the box and leading her cousin over to the chairs. She introduced Suzette and me, and after lots of hugs and expressions of sympathy, we all sat. Melanie gave the sign and one man started up the excavator while the other two stood nearby with shovels and straps. As the equipment scraped across the ground, Olive reached out and gripped her cousin's hand.

I'll give the Windy Oaks' staff credit, they were extremely careful and precise in their work. Dirt came up in the narrow bucket and was skillfully dumped into the wooden crate, ensuring the grass surrounding the plot was unsullied. The two men by the side loosened soil from the sides, their attention increasing as the excavator bucket sank lower into the ground.

The ghosts closed in, hovering over the gravesite. There were so many I couldn't tell who was male or female, or any distinguishing characteristics. All I knew was that they were agitated...angry.

I leaned over to Olive. "Are you...do you see, I mean feel, any of these...you know?"

She sucked in a breath. "I always have a hard time in cemeteries. Funeral homes and hospitals too. I try to block it all out, but yes, I know they're here."

"There's a lot," I murmured. "I visit my husband's grave sometimes, and I've never seen this many. Do you think it's because we're disturbing a grave? They seem...distraught."

A muscle in Olive's jaw twitched. "I'm sure that's got them stirred up. That and we do have a lot of emotions going on right now—both me and DeLanie. Ghosts are drawn to that sort of thing. Once David's moved, and Uncle Ford is buried, I'm sure they'll go back to wherever they were before."

I nodded and sat back, not wanting to upset her further by discussing it. Maybe she was right. Maybe it was just the emotion of what was happening, and the fact that one of their own was being moved. But something about these ghosts raised the hair on the back of my neck. I didn't feel like they were going to attack us or anything, but their anger....

It couldn't have been more than another five minutes when one of the men with the shovels gave a shout, thrusting his hand out in a gesture that clearly meant the man running the equipment should stop. I jumped, the yell out of place with the general tone of respect everyone had shown until that moment. The man running the digger shut off the power, and my ears rang with the sudden silence. It was then that I saw what had alarmed the man with the shovel. Right between the teeth of the excavator's bucket was a piece of bright blue plastic tarp, stained brown from the dirt.

"Are they ready to bring him up?" DeLanie asked, her voice unsteady. "So soon?"

Melanie came from behind us, walking over to where the three men were conversing as they glanced down into the plot. "They'll probably want to dig the rest by hand," she assured the other woman with a stiff smile. "They won't want to risk damaging the liner lid with the equipment."

Hadn't she seen the bit of tarp? She glanced at the blue caught in the digger's teeth, then down into the grave plot, her expression still bland. Yes, she had seen it. And clearly it didn't bother her. Melanie seemed completely unfazed. I knew she had a good poker face, but good grief. There was no reason for there to be a tarp in the grave dirt. I would have expected her to look panicked, mortified. Her calm demeanor shaken.

Maybe there was a good reason for that bit of torn blue. Maybe they put tarps on top of the caskets now? Certainly, David hadn't been buried with it in his casket. It wasn't likely the casket was rotted after six months. If the digger had accidently cut into it, there would have been a crack noise or something to indicate it had hit more than dirt.

Besides, weren't these graves all lined to keep the ground

from sinking? Yes, I distinctly remembered having to buy a grave liner when I buried Eli. Cemetery policy, Melanie had told me.

My heart beat a frantic rhythm. I plastered an expression on my face as close to Melanie's calm as I could. "Stay here," I told the other ladies as I got to my feet and walked over to where the men were clustered, their backs to us.

"We're only four feet in," one of them told Melanie in a hushed tone. "I stopped Paul as soon as I saw it."

"Maybe a mourning flag that got mixed in with the dirt," another man whispered. "Or someone snagged a section of the drape when they were filling it in. We're not that deep."

Melanie peered down into the grave, her face shifting from an expression of bland, calm sympathy and transforming into one of icy granite. "Get down there," she told one of the men. "Do the rest by hand."

"It's two more feet down," one man began to argue before another swatted him on the arm and with a warning glance, hopped down into the grave, shovel in hand. The second guy hopped down with them, while the third stood near the box that was to hold the dirt.

Melanie turned back to the others, the bland expression returning to her face. "It will be a bit longer. We're doing the remaining two feet by hand."

I eyed the scrap of blue on the bucket. As inappropriate as it would have been, I was tempted to reach out and pull it down to examine. The only thing besides impropriety that held me back was that the bucket was suspended over the grave plot, and I most likely would have fallen in trying to grab the shredded bit of tarp.

Glancing down, I saw it the same moment as the two men with the shovels. I saw it before the third man next to the dirt box, before Melanie who still had her back turned as she spoke to DeLanie. I saw it, and I realized we wouldn't be leaving anytime soon, that David's casket was most likely going to remain in this grave for a bit longer, that Uncle Ford might need to wait before he occupied the plot.

That scrap of tarp clawed up by the digger wasn't a mourning flag. It was a piece of tarp surrounding a body—a body lying four feet down in the grave without the benefit of a casket.

CHAPTER 5

*I*t didn't take the police long to arrive, right behind them the long van that I recognized as being from the Medical Examiner's office.

I realized the dark humor in my knowing what the M.E. van looked like. This wasn't the first body I'd seen. I'd gone my whole life without coming across a murder scene, and in one year I'd now encountered six. This was beginning to be an unwelcome habit of mine.

Was this why there were all these ghosts hovering over the grave? Why they were so angry? I squinted, trying to see if the figure-shaped shadows would become something more distinct. If anything, that just made them blurrier. It was frustrating. If I was going to have this odd ability to see the dead, it would help if I could truly see them. And communicate with them. As much as I didn't want to become that lady who went around talking to ghosts, it would make it a lot easier to find out what they wanted and how to get them to go away if we could speak to each other.

Two shadows separated from the mass, floating closer to

where we stood like a compact section of gray fog. One passed across Melanie and she shivered, rubbing her arms.

The manager had calmly halted the excavation and had informed us that she was shocked and embarrassed to say there appeared to be another body informally buried on top of David's casket. If that was her being shocked, I couldn't tell. The woman had an amazing poker face, but then again, I guess if you dealt with grieving people and remains all day, you'd be rather stoic about the whole thing. After apologizing profusely and letting us know that the relocation of David's remains would have to wait until this "issue" was resolved, she'd called the police.

I'd given Suzette the keys to my car, telling her to take DeLanie and Olive back to her house. Neither one of the women needed to be here to see this, and both clearly needed a stiff drink right now. Suzette had turned on the motherly instinct and headed off with the pair after making me promise I'd go over to her house to update them all as soon as things were wrapped up here.

It wasn't until they were gone that I realized that they were in my car and I hadn't grabbed either Olive's or DeLanie's keys to drive one of theirs. Thinking the police might be a bit too busy to drive me home and unsure about calling an Uber to a cemetery on a Saturday evening, I texted Judge Beck.

There's a dead body on top of the casket at Windy Oaks. Can you meet me here and give me a ride to Suzette's?

It took Judge Beck a while to respond, so I watched the cops take pictures of the crime scene, making sure they noticed the scrap of fabric at the edge of the bucket. I was certain the gravedigger men had let them know, but just in case I felt like I needed to point that out.

My phone beeped.

WHAT???

I thought I'd made it quite clear what was going on, but evidently Judge Beck needed some additional explanation. Honestly, he should have been used to my odd habit of discovering murder victims by now.

Murder. I was certain this person who'd been buried in a grave he didn't belong in had been murdered. It wasn't just the ghosts that swarmed around the gravesite; it was simple logic. There was no way someone would have wrapped themselves in a plastic blue tarp, accidently fallen into an open grave, and been accidentally covered over with dirt. Someone had put this body there. And whoever filled in the grave must have known there was an additional resident in the plot.

I texted the judge back. *Olive's family feud came to a head. DeLanie's son was to be moved. We were here, and as they were digging, they uncovered a body... Not in a casket.*

There. That was clear as…. dirt.

The police finished taking pictures. They'd strewn crime scene tape around the area, spoken to Melanie who had assured them that the canopy would remain up to not only protect evidence, but keep a half-open grave from filling in with rainwater and damaging the casket and remains that they still needed to exhume.

The Deputy—not Miles; he'd be so disappointed this hadn't happened early enough to get him out of the golf tourney—told Melanie that they hoped to be able to clear the crime scene by mid-week at the latest, so they could resume whatever they needed to do here.

Satisfied, Melanie stepped back and watched as two women hopped into the grave with small shovels, a box of plastic bags, and cameras. Two deputies stood up top next to a stretcher and straps, ready to bring the body up when the two women were done processing the evidence and unearthing the remains.

My phone beeped.

Why?

Why are you watching an exhumation? Did the casket come apart or something? Wasn't he just buried six months ago? And isn't there a vault or a liner or something?

I sighed and typed the equivalent of a short novel, explaining the entire thing. Texting wasn't the medium for this sort of lengthy dialogue, but it seemed Judge Beck couldn't wait until he'd actually arrived to learn the details.

By the time I'd finished and hit send, I saw the judge's SUV pull up behind the police cars. He was reading the text as he strode across the grass, his long black coat oddly reminiscent of his official robes. The deputies looked up at him. One stepped forward, only to recognize him at the last moment.

"Judge Beck," he stammered. "Can I help you? Is there something I can do…?"

The judge looked up at him, and I saw he had his professional expression on. Where Melanie's professional expression was cool, efficient, comforting, someone you could rely on in your time of need to dot all the i's and cross all the t's without fuss or muss, Judge Beck's would peel the paint from the side of a building. It too was cool and efficient, but it sliced like a laser. It made powerful men shake in their boots. It was incredibly intimidating. And sexy.

It was a bit embarrassing to realize that.

"I'm here to give Mrs. Carerra a ride home," he said, his voice like polished glass. "You can rest easy that I won't compromise your crime scene in any way."

The deputy gulped. "No, of course not, sir."

He stood aside and the judge walked toward me. He didn't look happy.

"I'm so sorry," I told him. "If it was a bother, I could have called Matt or someone else. I didn't mean to put you out like this."

He stopped in his tracks and blinked, the stern expression fading. "Kay, I'm not mad. I *want* you to call me if you need something like a ride...or anything, actually. I'm just... I'm worried. How many bodies have you found this year? That party planner. The man across the street. Holt Dupree. That vampire romance writer. And now this? Is this kind of thing common with you, or was my moving in a curse or something?"

I squirmed, not wanting to tell him about how I saw ghosts. Admittedly, a good number of my murder-victim discoveries would have happened even if I hadn't been able to see ghosts, but still...

"The party planner was the first," I confessed. "But I'd been taking care of Eli for ten years prior to that, so it's not like I got out a lot. It's not a curse. It's not you. It just seems to happen, and I'm going to go with it."

He sighed and ran a hand through his hair. "Poor Olive. How did she get roped into this?"

"I'm glad she did in a way," I told him. "This is DeLanie's son's grave. Can you imagine how dreadful this is for her? She's badgered by her cousin into moving her son's remains and comes here for what's clearly going to be an emotional event, only to have this happen? Having a sympathetic family member like Olive here helped. And now they're all over at Suzette's drinking wine and hopefully mending fences between the two sides of their family. I hate to think that she might have been here alone for this. Or with this Aunt Sarah that seems to hate her for some reason."

Judge Beck nodded. "You're right. I'm glad she wasn't alone. I just wish it wasn't always *you* in the middle of it all, Kay. I worry."

It warmed my heart to know he worried. "I know. And

I'm sorry, but this is who I am. I might not have been stumbling across bodies back in my journalism days, but I met with a lot of unsavory characters. Eli used to worry as well, but he knew he had to accept me as I was."

I cringed, realizing that I'd just compared him to Eli as if they had anywhere near the same relationship with me. Eli had been...well, he'd been my life, my partner, my lover, my until-death-do-us-part. Judge Beck was a tenant and a friend. A very close friend. But that was it.

Or was it?

The two women handed their cameras and several labeled plastic bags up to the deputies, then lowered the stretcher into the grave. Several bags of dirt came up, then the deputies hauled the body up on the stretcher. It was covered in a torn blue tarp. The two women guided the stretcher to the grass. Then while the deputies loaded it into the waiting van, the women continued bagging additional samples.

I eyed the sun low on the horizon and the darkening sky.

"Are you done here?" Judge Beck murmured. "Have you given a statement? Any additional graves you need to dig up while there's still some daylight?"

The two women began climbing up out of the grave. "I think I'm done here. There's nothing more for me to do until the medical examiner gets a look at things."

He rolled his eyes. "There's nothing more for you to do period besides go comfort your friend. Really Kay, leave this one for the police."

I stared at him, eyebrows raised. He grinned and let out an exaggerated sigh.

"Okay. Come on, Nancy Drew. Let's get you home." Judge Beck put a hand around my shoulders and steered me toward his SUV. "I'm sure you'll be knee-deep in all this by tomorrow morning and have the culprit in hand by the end of the week."

Maybe he did know me after all. "I need to find out who was killed and buried in that grave. And clearly whoever filled it in has to be complicit, don't you agree? I mean, how could you possibly fill in a grave without realizing there was a body tossed on top of the casket? The body was four feet down. If I figure in the depth of the casket, someone literally tossed him in on top, then covered him up. I'll need to talk to the cemetery manager and caretaker, and the gravediggers. Who was he? Was this just a convenient spot to dump his body, or was there some reason he was put in a grave plot with David?"

Judge Beck stuffed me into the passenger seat of his vehicle then went around to the other side, his face filled with amusement.

"I'm sure you'll get to the bottom of it, Kay. In the meantime, you've had a busy day, and I'm pretty sure you haven't had dinner yet. Steak? Chinese? That new sushi place out by Milford?"

"I told Suzette I'd get back to her place and let Olive and DeLanie know what happened." I bit my lip, thinking that dinner *would* be nice right now. Had Suzette ordered pizza? Would there be any left?

Crap! The cemetery would close at sunset and both Olive's and DeLanie's cars were still inside. Was there an after-hours number to call to open the gate? Or maybe they could just stay at Suzette's or my house, and we'd take them over in the morning.

How horrible for this to happen to DeLanie. I'd just met the woman and already my heart ached for her. To have lost her son, then been pressured by her cousin into moving his remains only to have a murder victim unearthed on top of his casket. Poor DeLanie. And poor Olive.

"Takeout," Judge Beck announced. "We're going to grab some tacos at a drive-though, then the pair of us are going over to Suzette's house."

"The pair of us?" I asked, wondering if he hadn't meant he was intending on dropping me off. I could walk home. Suzette was only a block away from me.

"The pair of us," he assured me. "Because in spite of my lecturing you back there, I'm curious. I'd also really like to know how that body got buried with your friend's cousin."

I fastened my seatbelt and turned to him. "Suzette was going to order pizza. Let's just head there, and if she didn't get anything, we can order delivery ourselves."

"Pizza it is."

We followed the M.E. van out of the cemetery, the gates closing firmly behind us.

"So, how'd your team do in the golf tourney?" I asked, eager to lighten the mood a bit.

"Second place." The judge seemed especially pleased about that. "We all got ribbons. I'll show you mine when we get home. I'm thinking of sticking it on the refrigerator like we used to do with the kids' grade school artwork."

"Go right ahead. The fridge could use some decoration. So, who won?"

He sniffed. "The Hole-In-One-Listing team, who else?"

I laughed. "Those real estate ladies? They win everything."

"I know. If I ever need to buy or sell a house, I'm definitely using them."

The smile froze on my face. Was he planning on buying a house soon? I wanted to ask, but I didn't want to either imply that I was eager for him to move or that I was worried he would. It was the latter that bothered me the most, sending me closer to a panic attack than catching a glimpse of a body in that grave plot.

"Well, I'm assuming you and Heather will eventually sell your house," I said instead.

His expression soured. "Eventually is the key word there. I want to sell the house and move on, but Heather's digging in her heels. She's pushing to keep it, even though there's no way she can afford the mortgage. She can't afford it even *without* buying me out of my share, let alone after."

"I don't know much about divorce, but most couples seem to end up selling the house," I told him. "I'm sure your lawyers will hash it all out."

"For what I'm paying my lawyer, I hope so," he commented dryly. "I certainly don't want it. It's a nice house, but it's bigger than we needed and was stupidly expensive. Looking back, it wasn't the smartest decision to buy it."

"Why did you?" I asked, half expecting him to blame Heather and say she'd pressured him into it. I actually liked Judge Beck's soon-to-be ex-wife. She seemed to enjoy her luxuries, but didn't appear to be one of those people who desperately needed to keep up with the uber-rich Joneses.

"My career, that's why," was his surprising answer.

"Impressing the partners at your former law firm?" I guessed.

He nodded. "It wasn't just that, though. I've always wanted to be a judge but being appointed is a bit who you know, a bit your professional reputation, and a bit how you present yourself. Ever since high school, I've been leveraging the connections my parents had as well as connections I made in college. I made sure I had the right internships, the right law school, and even the right law firm for a first job."

"The right country club, the right parties, the right house in the right neighborhood," I added. "The right golf swing."

He shot me a smirk. "I'll have you know my putting game was spot-on today."

"Supreme Court here you come," I teased.

"I wish. I don't have those kinds of connections, though, and probably never will. Now Henry or Madison, if they go into law, might be able to springboard off what I've done and reach that high."

"Madison's going to be a chef/anthropologist/softball player, and Henry is going to have one of those antique evaluation shows on television. I think you'll have to do the Supreme Court route yourself."

He was silent for a moment and I began to worry that my teasing had insulted him or made him sad that neither child would follow in his footsteps. They were still young. They might change their minds. I know I did at that age—clearly since I'd never become a foreign ambassador.

"Can I share something with you in confidence?" he finally asked.

"Of course." A thrill ran through me at the thought.

"There's some talk about me being considered for an appellate judgeship at the state level."

"That's amazing," I said, all the while I calculated the distance from Locust Point to the capital, realizing that he'd hardly want to commute nearly two hours each way five days a week.

The kids. Was this why he had been pushing for primary custody? This one week on and one week off wouldn't work in school districts two hours apart. If he did get primary custody and moved, how would the kids feel about having to switch schools? Or only seeing their mom every other weekend? And what if he didn't get custody? In spite of everything he'd told me about changing his life to make his children more of a priority, would he end up putting his career first? Was this the sort of offer he just couldn't refuse, even if it meant less time with Madison and Henry?

"There are logistical issues if it happens," he admitted, as if he'd read my mind. "Serious logistical issues. I'm flattered they're even considering me. To be an appellate judge at that level…I'd be working with the other judges to set legal precedents in the state to review death-row appeals. It's an exciting opportunity."

I nodded. "No more juries. No more trials. Just listening to oral arguments, reviewing case law, and deciding with a group of other judges. Writing opinion papers and that sort of thing. It'd be very different from what you're doing now."

"True, very different. I'd still be making an impact, but at a higher level. And I can't deny that I'm thrilled they're even considering me. I'm young for a judge as it is. I'd be especially young for an appellate court judge." He glanced over at me. "Depending on what cases come my way, if I get this appointment I could end up being considered for a federal judgeship at some point."

"And then a Supreme Court nomination," I teased.

He rolled his eyes. "That's not going to happen. The opportunity in front of me might not even happen. There are lots of qualified judges in the state—ones who've been on the bench a lot longer than I have. It's an honor to even be approached about a nomination, and I feel like I need to pursue it. Just in case."

Understanding that if he got an offer, he'd cross that bridge when he came to it. I took a breath, realizing what a huge crossroads this would be for him. If he got the offer and ended up refusing it because of the custody situation, he'd most likely never be considered again. It wouldn't be the end of the world. His current appointment was pretty close to a lifetime one. Every eight years, his name got stuck on the ballot for what was basically a confidence vote. I didn't recall there ever being a judge that got voted off. People tended to just check that box and move on to the more contentious political offices up for vote. He'd keep his current Circuit Court judgeship.

But that would most likely be where he career stayed for the rest of his life. And I got the idea that would be difficult for Judge Beck to accept.

Eli had been absolutely dedicated to his career, but as a surgeon, he hadn't needed to do quite the mover-and-shaker political dance that Judge Beck had. And success in Eli's mind had always been about solving a challenging medical problem, helping to make sure his patients had the best life they could. I knew Judge Beck cared about delivering justice to the people who came into his courtroom, but he also had a personal ambition that was very different from Eli's.

"So, what goes into you getting a nomination?" I asked, curious about the process. "Did you preside over a controversial case this past year or something?"

"Professional experience does play into a nomination, but sadly it's mostly networking that gets someone noticed," he admitted. "Attending events. Fundraisers. Keeping in touch with people you went to school with or worked with and their connections. Family connections play into it as well. Then there's politics, sadly. Are you conservative in your rulings and opinion papers, or more liberal? Does that align with the current state or federal government representatives and their leanings? Reputation also matters. It helps to drink with the right people, but always having a martini in hand means you're a bit of a risk to recommend. Same with gambling, financial issues, marital issues."

"Marital issues?" I winced, worried that the judge's current "marital issues" might derail his career aspirations.

"Divorce is okay, as long as it's not so ugly that there is dirty laundry flying in the wind. Things like rumors of unusual sexual practices, abuse allegations, and that sort of thing can get your name off the list."

"Mistresses," I added.

He grimaced. "Sadly, that's not a deal breaker as long as it's discreet."

I remembered that Judge Beck had told me he'd never cheated on Heather. I'd asked once, and as rude as it sounded now to have pried like that, we'd been talking about his divorce and his reply had been a moment of honesty on his part.

Actually, Judge Beck had always been honest with me. And far more forthright about the details of his personal life than I'd ever expected. That first day I'd met him, he'd seem so reserved and guarded. I got the feeling he was that way with most people—friendly, but in a formal sort of way with firm boundaries. Maybe it was our friendship, maybe it was living in close quarters with each other these last seven months, but he never seemed to hold back anything from me.

And the only thing I held back from him was my seeing ghosts. Maybe someday I'd tell him when I was sure he wouldn't think I was having a mental health crisis. Maybe...

CHAPTER 6

The judge drove past our house and to the end of the street where Suzette's cabin sat down a long lane. Our houses were all built on what had once been her family's land. She'd inherited the cabin from her grandparents along with the remaining acreage of what had been a huge farm.

The cabin had originally been a small, one-room structure with a loft overhead for sleeping quarters. Over the last two centuries, it had expanded here and there in odd clapboard additions that added a first-floor bedroom, a kitchen with a dining area, and two bathrooms. It was still a small house, especially compared to the huge Victorian houses that lined the road, but it was quaint and cozy, and it had been clear from the moment I'd met her that Suzette wouldn't have wanted to live anywhere else.

Judge Beck pulled up behind my sedan, turned off the car, and began to climb out.

"You're really coming in?"

"There's pizza. It's Saturday. I've been playing golf most of the day and have nothing planned for tomorrow. I want to support Olive and her family. And I'll admit that I'm curious." He hesitated. "Unless this is a woman thing. Would me being there make everything awkward?"

I snorted. "More awkward than having your son's remains exhumed and the diggers finding another dead body in the grave? Come join us. If anything, having a legal mind there might help."

His eyebrows shot up as he came around the SUV to walk by my side. "A legal mind? I'm going to bolt if you gals are expecting me to weigh in on the legal perspective of any of this."

I looped my arm around his. "Relax. I meant a calm, logical approach. DeLanie is bound to be upset, and Olive as well. We're here to be sympathetic, supportive, and let everyone cry it out if they need to."

Suzette opened the door and the moment I walked in I realized that the three of them were a bit over the line of tipsy.

"Kay!" Suzette threw her arms around me. "Come in. Oh, and Judge Beck." Her voice immediately sobered. I noticed she didn't throw her arms around my companion.

"Hi, Suzette." He gave her a charming smile. "I gave Kay a ride from the cemetery. She said she'd promised to come here and update you all and talk about what happened. Is it okay if I join in?"

"Oh. Of course. Come in, come in." She turned bright red, obviously flustered. "White or red? Wine I mean, because we have wine. And we have hand-tossed veggie pizza or deep-dish pepperoni with extra cheese. Are you hungry?"

We walked in to find Olive and DeLanie sitting on the couch in front of a roaring fire, pizza and wine spread out all over the coffee table in front of them.

Both women stood and I introduced DeLanie to Judge Beck.

DeLanie twisted her hands together as she turned to me. "Is the cemetery...do you know if they're going to move David tomorrow?"

"I really don't know, but I'm sure that Melanie woman will call you as soon as they're given the okay to proceed. There's crime scene tape everywhere right now. They've got a tarp over the grave and the canopy. I'll drive you back tomorrow to get your car and we can ask when they think the police will release the scene."

"Who was that in the grave with David?" she asked. "Whose body was in there? And why David's grave?"

She'd been through so much, and now this. I reached out and gripped her hands in mine. "I don't know who it is yet. And it may not have anything to do with your son. It could have just been a convenient spot to hide a body. It could have been that his interment just happened to coincide with someone's murder. I'm so sorry this is happening to you. It's so unfair that you're going through all this."

"It is." Olive put her arm around her cousin's shoulders. "Losing David was hard enough. Having to move his remains...I'm so sorry, DeLanie. I love Aunt Sarah, but she's wrong about this. And I'm sure Uncle Ford would never have wanted you to go through this."

DeLanie nodded, pulling her hands from mine to wipe her eyes. "Ford was a good man. And Sarah...I know she's probably doing this because of a combination of grief and old resentment. It's just...having David buried away from the family section feels like he's being exiled. It feels like he's being shunned because of how he died."

My heart twisted.

"Everyone thinks of drug abuse as some sort of moral failing, a weakness of will. No wonder people hide it when they're struggling with an addiction." DeLanie shook her head. "I never saw anyone fight so hard against this as David.

He was a smart man. He went to college, had a good job, had everything. He wasn't weak; this thing just dug its claws into him and like a cancer, it wouldn't give up. He fought so hard, but ultimately it got the best of him. Sadly, people will always judge him by his death, not his life. People will always see him as a weak-willed junkie and not a bright, funny, wonderful man who gave recovery everything he could, but died anyway."

"That's not how anyone in the family thinks of David," Olive argued. "How he died…it was tragic, but his struggles don't negate the fact that he was a *good* man. Everyone in the family hoped he'd beat this. We were all rooting for him, DeLanie. And this stupid fight over the grave plot has nothing to do with how David died. I honestly don't know why Aunt Sarah is so fixated on having that plot, or why she's pushing to have David's remains moved, but her actions don't speak for the rest of us. And we *all* loved David."

Judge Beck stood silent in the background. I glanced over at him, thinking he'd probably seen his share of drug-related crime in his courtroom, and how addiction could ruin a life —a whole family.

DeLanie wiped her eyes again. "Twice before he'd been in rehab. This time…this time, I thought he was going to make it. He'd gotten a new job. He wasn't hanging out with his old friends anymore. He was going to meetings five times a week. He'd told me he had a sponsor who had been clean for more than ten years. I'd thought he was going to get married and I'd have a wedding to look forward to and grandkids. Then I get the call that night…"

DeLanie slumped down on the sofa. Olive sat beside her, holding her cousin and consoling her while the rest of us stood around in a sort of awkward sympathy. I could sympathize with her grief even though I'd never had children of my own, even though I'd never had any thoughts of grandkids or watching future generations live their lives. Looking up at Judge Beck, I could see from the expression on his face he was thinking of his own two kids and how he'd feel if *he* got that call in the middle of the night.

"Let's talk about the good times," Olive finally said. "You wanted David to be defined by his life, not his death, so let's let tonight be one of happy memories and a celebration of life, not of sorrow. We can't do anything about David's remains or that other body right now. Or about Uncle Ford. Let's try to think about the good things in life, no matter how short it might be, and drink to those who've gone before us."

Suzette started to fill wine glasses, pulling an extra two from a cabinet against the back wall. "It's not like anyone is going anywhere tonight with cars stuck in the cemetery and us drinking. I've got a spare bed up in the loft, and I can make up the couch into a place to sleep."

"I've got plenty of room at my house," I said, warming to the idea with Judge Beck's nod of approval. "Why don't you stay with us for the night. We're just down the street, and we've got two spare bedrooms made up and ready for a guest. There's apple muffins for breakfast, and I can drive you to get your car in the morning."

The woman blinked up at me. "Oh, I wouldn't want to put you out, dear. I've just met you!"

"You're Olive's cousin," I assured her. "Which means you're welcome to stay in my house. Olive can take the loft here, and you can have your pick of my two guest rooms."

"You're getting the better deal," Olive teased. "Kay makes the best muffins. Suzette's idea of breakfast is cold pork chops or instant oatmeal."

"Hey!" Suzette protested with a grin. "Sometimes I pick up a box of Pop-Tarts."

Olive rolled her eyes. "See?"

DeLanie laughed. "Okay. Thank you, Kay. Are you sure…"

Her gaze slid to Judge Beck. "You don't mind, sir?"

He smiled, toasting her with a glass of red wine. "I don't mind at all, DeLanie. As long as you leave a few apple muffins for me, you're absolutely welcome."

The woman took a deep breath, then smiled back, lifting her glass. "Then let's talk about the good memoires, starting with that time Olive and her brother convinced David that an entire bucket of frogs would be happy living in our bathtub."

Olive laughed. "Or when you made that cake for David's birthday and forgot to set the oven timer?"

DeLanie shook her head with a chuckle. "That thing was like a piece of charcoal."

"After you put the fire out," Olive added.

"Good thing I had time to run to the grocery store and buy a replacement."

"Good thing David didn't mind having a wedding cake for his birthday." Olive laughed.

And that was our night—all of us telling stories about our childhood as we ate pizza and drank wine. And then at the end of the night, we left all the cars in Suzette's driveway while Judge Beck, DeLanie, and I walked back to my house. DeLanie was quickly settled into the third-floor guest room —the one that included a sitting area in the turret and exposed oak beams along the ceiling. I went down to set up the coffee on an automatic timer and noticed Taco standing over his food bowl, a reproachful expression on his face.

Oh no. My poor cat. Not that he was starving to death or anything, but I was a horrible cat-mom for having forgotten his dinner.

"I fed him, you know."

I jumped at Judge Beck's voice in the doorway and nearly spilled the bag of cat food across the floor. Taco sprang upon the few nuggets that fell.

"Thank you. I was feeling guilty about being so late at getting him his dinner."

The judge leaned back against the doorjamb, folding his arms across his chest. He'd changed into a pair of pajama bottoms with Pac-Mans all over them and a worn T-shirt advertising some brew pub that had gone out of business ten years ago.

"What are you doing tomorrow, Kay? After you take DeLanie back to her car, that is."

His voice was deep with a sort of resonance that reminded me of when Taco purred. Maybe it was the wine. Maybe it was the emotion-laden tone of the evening. Maybe it was something else, but I suddenly wanted a man's arms around me.

I pushed that idea away and considered the judge's question. I *had* thought after dropping DeLanie off, I'd pop over to the Legion and help Matt tally up numbers from the golf tourney, but that thought went right out of my head.

"I don't have any plans. Heather drops the kids off at four, doesn't she?"

He nodded, unfolding his arms and taking a few steps toward me. "At five. Let's go have brunch. Then maybe go to a pumpkin patch."

"A pumpkin patch?" I squeaked. "To buy pumpkins?" It must be the wine because my mind felt totally scrambled.

"And go through the corn maze." He took another step forward, his gaze intent. "It's a big corn maze. They've got hot cider, and goats you can feed, and we can take the hay wagon out to the pumpkin patch and pick out what we want. We'll buy some carving tools and come back and make jack-o'-lanterns. Halloween is Thursday, you know. We should decorate. And get candy for trick-or-treaters. Do you get trick-or-treaters here?"

I suddenly felt as if I couldn't breathe. "Yes, we do. But

you don't want to wait until Madison and Henry get here and all of us go to the pumpkin patch together?"

"No, I want to go with you. Just us. We can get pumpkins with Madison and Henry another time if they want. Tomorrow…I want it to just be us."

I focused really hard on taking slow steady breaths. It had been almost a decade since I'd carved pumpkins, and longer since I'd actually gone to the pumpkin patch to pick them out. Years.

"I'd like that. It sounds like fun." I shifted the bag of cat food in my arms, then realizing I was still clutching it, I stuffed it back into the cabinet, much to Taco's chagrin.

Judge Beck stooped down and picked the cat up in his arms. "Piggy. You've already eaten, and you weigh more than some dogs I know."

Taco nestled into his arms, purring like a motor and rubbing his head against the judge's bicep. I felt a sudden stab of envy. Then a stab of guilt.

Where was Eli's ghost? He was usually that comforting presence in the house at night, but I hadn't sensed the spirit since I'd returned from Suzette's. Walking around the kitchen island, I reached out to take Taco from the judge's arms, feeling a zing at the brush of my arm against his.

"I'll see you in the morning then," I murmured, feeling suddenly sweaty, warmer than the worst hot flash, and torn between wanting to escape to my room and do something I'd be mortified about come morning.

"See you then," he murmured back.

I escaped, trying not to run, not to squeeze Taco too tight as I climbed the stairs to my bed and a night of restless dreams that jumbled together Eli and the man who was asleep one floor directly below me.

CHAPTER 7

I was up before the sun, missing Daisy as I performed my backyard yoga solo. It had dipped down to freezing in the night, and my breath plumed out in front of me as I did my poses. Yoga wasn't exactly an aerobic activity, and even with heavy-duty tights and a long-sleeved shirt, I was cold and rushing a bit to finish up. When Daisy returned, I was going to suggest we move our morning exercise to my basement until spring and warmer weather returned.

After I'd finished, I jogged around the front of the house to retrieve my paper from where the nameless delivery woman had thrown it from the window of her station wagon. It was a bit of a hunt, but this morning the paper was clearly visible half sticking out of my boxwood. Jogging back to the rear entrance of my house because I was too darned cold to try to unlock my front door, I dashed inside to the welcome warmth and the tantalizing scent of fresh brewed coffee. Relishing the time alone, I sat at the counter with my hot coffee and spread out the paper.

Yes, paper. I spent enough of my day clicking through the

internet. Getting my news the traditional way allowed me to be that old woman with an actual newspaper at the breakfast table. Or kitchen island, as it was.

The joy of small-town newspapers was that the local stuff was front and center, with important state and national news taking a less prominent spot below the fold, or even back in the back sections. Sure enough, right next to the lead article about last night's high school basketball game—priorities— was the headline *Extra Body Found in Local Grave*. The sub header announced that the police suspected murder.

Well, duh. As I'd speculated last night, the guy was hardly wandering around the cemetery wrapped in a blue tarp, only to fall into an open grave. Although I guess that sort of thing *was* technically possible. Glancing through the article, I realized I'd made a glaring error.

The body was that of a woman.

A chill crept over me, one the hot strong coffee couldn't ease. I sensed something in the corner of the kitchen, a shadowy form that wasn't the one I'd come to think of as my husband.

Another ghost. A woman. Young. Upset. Needing my help.

I should have known from the moment those men had uncovered the body that I'd get a visit from a ghost. Judge Beck had noted that I seemed to be especially adept at coming across murder victims, but little did he know I also seemed to draw their ghosts to me. And past experience told me this spirit wouldn't rest until her murderer was found and brought to justice.

I read on, trying to ignore the ghost in my kitchen. The paper said the woman had died from an apparent gunshot wound to the chest, although the police had told the reporter they wouldn't be able to announce anything else until the medical examiner took a look. Gunshot wound. So this definitely was a body dump because I couldn't see some woman wandering around the cemetery being shot conveniently in front of a grave and falling backward into it.

I shivered again from a combination of the ghost in my kitchen and the thought of a gruesome execution.

A woman, not a man as I'd originally thought. That bothered me. I'd assumed the body was a man's and the idea that a woman had been killed and tossed in the grave seemed more frightening than if the victim had been the other gender. I frowned, thinking of the press of spirits I'd felt around the grave while they'd been digging for David's casket. They'd been angry. Upset. Maybe they weren't so stirred up over the disturbance to David's remains as the fact that a murder victim was being unearthed.

Maybe the anger I'd felt was a need for vengeance, a desire for one of their own to have some justice when it came to her murder. And with the body being unearthed, justice did seem like a possibility now.

And the two that had pulled free from the group to whisk around the grave plot...had one of them been this woman's ghost? The ghost in my kitchen? A few of the spirits I'd encountered did seem to stick around where their bodies were, but others remained close to the place they'd been murdered. Some just seemed to wander around, latching onto items of significance, or even following me around once they realized I could sense them, like this one.

Like Holt. Who thankfully hadn't been here since football season started. Was it bad that I hoped he was hanging around the team locker rooms and would be far more interested in his favorite sport than in gluing himself to a sixty-year-old woman?

"Who are you?" I murmured to the ghost, wishing for once that I had Olive's ability to communicate with the dead. I didn't want to upset my friend by enlisting her help in this one, not when she had to deal with her uncle's death and the family drama. True, this woman had been buried in with Olive's cousin, but that was probably the only connection. It had been a coincidence, a convenient dump site for a body. No doubt the murderer was connected somehow with the gravediggers, or the cemetery, or had been burying a family member or friend nearby when a fatal argument broke out, or...

Why *had* her murderer decided to put her in a grave as opposed to just leaving her in an alleyway, or in the woods, or at the bottom of a pond? Someone had wanted to hide the body. And although hiding a body in a cemetery grave seemed like a brilliant idea, it would have required some cooperation with either the cemetery personnel and/or the people who were in charge of filling in the gravesites.

Which meant there had to be a connection somewhere. I thought of Melanie and wondered if she was harboring any deep dark secrets. Probably not. If she'd been the one who killed this woman, I couldn't believe she would have been so calm and collected during the early part of the exhumation.

Unless her poker face really was that good.

"Morning!" a voice called from the dining room.

The ghost vanished with the word. Gone. Poof. I looked up to see DeLanie walk into the kitchen. I'd loaned her some pajamas, but she'd obviously washed up and changed back into her clothing from yesterday.

"Morning," I returned her greeting. "Coffee is over there. Help yourself. I'll get the muffins out, then if you don't mind, I'll run up for a quick shower and to change out of my workout clothes."

"No hurry." She smiled at me as she headed over toward the coffee. "Whatever your schedule, I'm good. I really appreciate you letting me stay last night and giving me a lift over to my car this morning. And the muffins, which I'm sure are amazing. Olive is lucky to have such wonderful friends."

If DeLanie was feeling a little awkward or maybe a bit hungover in the light of day, she sure didn't show it. The woman had a strained, tight look about her face, but that was understandable given what had happened last night. Determined not to rub salt in the wound, I flipped over the paper and stuffed it under a basket of fruit, got out the muffins, and once again told my guest that she was free to help herself to anything. Then I headed upstairs to shower and change.

When I came down, DeLanie was finishing the last of her coffee, a handful of muffin foils on a plate beside an open newspaper. Although she must have read the news about the body, she didn't bring it up and neither did I. We walked up to Suzette's for my car and I managed to squeeze it around Judge Beck's SUV, noting that no one in the cabin seemed to be stirring. It wasn't surprising. Suzette wasn't an early riser, and everyone had had an emotional, long day yesterday.

We drove most of the way to the cemetery in silence, pulling through the gates and navigating the winding lanes through the sections to where DeLanie's family plots were located.

"The police tape is still there," she commented softly as the canopy and tarps came into view.

"It's Sunday," I reminded her. "The police will probably keep it as a crime scene until midweek to give the forensic people and the medical examiner's office a while to process everything."

"I just want it over with," she told me. "I want David settled in his new home with the head stone and everything proper-like. I know he wouldn't have cared. I know he wouldn't have wanted me to be crying and worrying over his body like this. I just wanted him with family. I didn't want to feel like he was an outcast."

I reached over to grab her hand. "He's not an outcast. The cemetery is full of generation after generation of loved ones. And the new section where he's going to be moved? Eli's there. My husband. I buried him the month before you lost your son."

DeLanie turned her hand in mine and squeezed my fingers. "Oh, hon, I'm so sorry. I just assumed that you and the judge…"

I blinked away sudden tears. "My husband died this past spring. Eli Carrera. He was a surgeon, practicing until his accident ten years ago. We don't have family locally, so I bought a plot for him when he died. But I want you to know that he'd welcome your son. If you're worried about that sort of thing, about him being all alone out in a different section, Eli would welcome him. He was like that. He was that sort of man."

"Thank you." She gave my hand another squeeze. "I know it's silly, but that does make me feel better to know David will be among friends. Maybe family is more than those you're related by blood to. Maybe family is something you build."

It was a sentiment I'd thought about quite a bit in the last seven months. I pulled up next to DeLanie's car and dug a business card out of my purse. "If you need anything, please give me a call. This is my work number, but Olive has my home phone and so does Suzette, and you know where I live."

"Thank you." She took the card and glanced down at it. "Pierson Investigations. Well, one thing you could do for me is to let me know if you find anything out about the body they discovered in my son's grave. I feel a bit responsible to follow up on that, you know."

I nodded, knowing exactly how she felt. "I'll contact you, although I doubt the police will release any additional information for a few days—or weeks if the M.E.'s office is backed up. So far the only thing that's being reported is that the body was that of a woman and she died of a gunshot wound."

DeLanie recoiled at that, making me realize that she must not have read the front page of the paper after all. Her brown eyes blinked at me for a moment as she pulled herself together. "A woman?"

"Does that mean anything to you?" I winced, realizing that I sounded less than sympathetic. "I mean, I'm sure her being in David's grave was just a coincidence, a convenient place to dispose of a body. I'm sure it has nothing to do with your son at all. I just wondered…."

She shook her head, pocketing my card and opening the car door. "No. I'm just shocked. I guess I thought it was a man's body down there. I never thought that a woman might…. Although I know women are murdered plenty often enough." She exited my car and turned to me, a forced smile on her face. "Thank you again, Kay. Olive speaks very highly of you, and I can see why. I appreciate your kindness and hospitality."

And with that, she was gone. I watched her start her car and back around, driving down the road to exit the cemetery before I put my sedan in park and got out, walking to the edge of where the police crime-scene tape had been stretched.

Ghosts. Their shadowy forms darted here and there as they clustered around David's plot. Once again, I struggled to separate and glimpse their personalities and forms from each other. One hovered over the gravesite, and I walked closer, getting the impression that spirit was David. He felt young. Definitely male. And…sad. He was awash in guilt and regret for the sorrow he'd left behind. And he seemed unable to leave the spot where his body had been interred. The ghost

I'd sensed in my kitchen appeared, hovering next to him by the grave.

Who was she, this woman who'd been shot...murdered? And just as important, who had killed her and arranged to hide her body in David's grave?

CHAPTER 8

There was no sign of Judge Beck when I got home, so I made another pot of coffee, let Taco outside, and sat on the porch with my laptop and a cup of coffee.

It was a darned chilly morning, but with that glorious fall sunshine that makes a person feel like summer is hanging on with every last breath. The maple out front was a brilliant red, and the Miller's tulip poplars were beginning to shed green-gold leaves. Fall had come late to Locust Point this year, and that was fine with me. I'd miss these weekends on the porch with my coffee. I'd miss the happy hours with the neighbors. And sunrise yoga with Daisy would be an issue depending on how cold it got this winter. Neither of us wanted to attempt Sun Salutations while bundled up in parkas, or in a foot of snow, but somehow yoga in my basement never felt the same.

But I wasn't going to think about that now. Instead I sipped my coffee, watched Taco stalking something or another in the mums, and opened my laptop.

David Driver. I eyed the obituary, noting that in the list of surviving relatives, he was DeLanie's only child, and that there was no father mentioned, either living or deceased. It made me feel even sorrier for the woman I'd just dropped off at the cemetery. Olive, her brother, and her parents were listed as surviving relatives in the obituary, as were Sarah, Ford, and their two children. David had been a very good-looking man from the picture in the notice—short dark tightly-curled hair, high cheekbones and an angular jaw, dark eyes and a mischievous, little-boy smile. If I'd been a young woman, and this man had turned that smile on me, I would have been absolutely charmed. Smitten, even.

Beyond the usual information regarding surviving relatives, there was a summary of the deceased's life—high school, college. David had worked at Branch Building and Electric. He'd been a member of Trinity Lutheran Church. He loved white water rafting and fishing, as well as his bulldog, Beau. In lieu of flowers, the family had requested donations to the local animal shelter that David had adopted Beau from.

I took a breath, feeling a bit raw, remembering how I'd had to write an obituary seven months ago. I watched Taco scamper across the lawn to roll in a patch of sunshine, banishing those memories before turning to my laptop to search further.

David Driver might have died from a drug overdose but there was no record of him ever being arrested or serving time for anything, including anything drug related. There were a few traffic tickets from three and six years ago. Nothing else appeared on my case search. The local newspaper had a few mentions of him in their archives—one of him at age four with his mother at the county fair and another as part of a winning Little League team. Other than that, there was nothing. David Driver had been a normal man who had tragically been caught up in a web of addiction and died before he could break free.

I heard the squeak of the front door.

"Sorry. I can't believe I slept in this late." Judge Beck sat down in the chair next to me, a cup of coffee in one hand and an apple muffin in the other. He was still wearing the Pac-Man pajama pants and the worn T-shirt.

"I guess golf takes a lot out of a man," I teased.

"I'm not getting any younger." He laughed. "Although I think it was less the eighteen holes and more the wine that had me sleeping in so late."

"You're hung over?"

He shot me a sideways scowl. "The Honorable Nathaniel Beck does not get hung over. Well, not since that time in college. And the bachelor party. And that New Year's Eve a few years back."

I smirked, thinking there had probably been a few other times he'd not mentioned. It wasn't a big deal. I wasn't exactly a stranger to parties, although it had been more than a few years since I'd imbibed enough to be what I'd call hungover.

"Lightweight. We can always skip the pumpkin patch if you'd rather lie on the couch with an ice pack on your head or something."

"Nope. Brunch, then pumpkin patch, then carving time." He pointed a finger at me. "You're not getting out of this."

I sipped my coffee. "Bloody Marys with brunch? Mimosas?"

He winced. "Give me a couple of cups of coffee and maybe I'll think about a virgin Bloody Mary. What's up with the laptop? It's Sunday. I thought *I* was the workaholic here."

"Just checking DeLanie's son's records." I shrugged. "No arrests. Nothing. I can't see any obvious reason why someone would have dumped a woman's body into his grave. At least from what I see in the papers or his obit."

Judge Beck finished his muffin and took a swig from his coffee cup. "I'm no cop, but the first place I'd check is the cemetery. Who filled that grave in? I can't believe someone didn't notice a body wrapped in a tarp on top of the casket."

"Grave liner." I turned my laptop around to show him the picture. "Evidently every grave in the last fifty years at Windy Oaks has either a vault or a grave liner. When they open the plot, basically they dig the hole, then they install the grave liner. After the service, they lower the casket, place the lid on the grave liner, then fill in the dirt on top."

He shrugged. "Still the same issue. Someone filling in that grave was either complicit, or your murderer. Either they did the deed and used their job as a way to cover it up, or they were paid to turn the other way for a disposal."

"It might have nothing to do with David Driver." I closed the laptop and shook my head. "Poor DeLanie has been through enough. I'll admit that I was worried her son's death and this body could be somehow connected."

"Because he died of a drug overdose?" Judge Beck turned a knowing glance my way. "You wouldn't be the first to think that, but plenty of addicts manage to skirt that line and remain fairly functioning. Not all of them end up robbing houses and living in flop houses."

"I didn't mean that," I protested. "I just thought that maybe...I don't know, people that use drugs might associate with those who could do something like murder?"

"Not always. I had a case a few years back where a college-educated soccer mom got arrested with a bottle of prescription drugs that weren't hers. She'd meet her dealer outside the grocery store. None of these people were your stereotypical boys-in-the-hood. Her dealer was a suburban grandmother. This thing could be drug related, or it could just be a coincidence that someone chose your friend's cousin's grave to hide a body." He reached out and tapped the top of my laptop. "Now go get ready. I want brunch. And a virgin Bloody Mary."

I stood, gathering my coffee cup and computer. "You're the one still in your pajamas, buster. You go get ready. I'll have another cup of coffee and see if I can find where Taco ran off to."

By the time I'd tracked my cat down, taunting the neighbor's dog, and hauled him back home, Judge Beck was ready.

I've had a lot of wonderful days in my life, and this counted as one of them. We went to brunch at an amazing place in downtown Milford and had pecan and caramel French toast, thick slabs of crispy applewood-smoked bacon, and mimosas. Fat and happy, we hit the pumpkin patch, forking out five dollars' worth of quarters to feed goats and donkeys handfuls of sweetened grain before moving on to the other attractions. The corn maze was horror-movie worthy. After staggering through rustling eight-foot-high stalks, we managed to find the exit and rewarded ourselves with some hot apple cider before boarding a hay wagon to the pumpkin field. Half an hour later, we were standing in a long line with a wheelbarrow that held two giant pumpkins and a dozen warty decorative gourds that I couldn't resist picking up.

"Wait here," Judge Beck told me before vanishing into the crowd. I inched my way toward the cashier, pushing the wheelbarrow and adding a couple more interesting gourds and mini pumpkins from the displays to my left. When the judge returned, he deposited a handful of pumpkin carving tools into the wheelbarrow along with a gallon of apple cider and a box of pumpkin spice donuts.

I stared at the donuts, feeling a bit insulted. "You've got

to be kidding me. Did you not just eat my apple muffins this morning? My lemon zest pound cake earlier in the week? My banana-walnut pancakes? You dare to deposit some other person's baked goods into my cart...wheelbarrow?"

He looked back at the section where the baked goods were displayed. "They're homemade. I'm not cheating on you if I eat other people's baked goods, am I? Because I figured it might be nice for you to get out of the kitchen for a hot second and spend some time carving pumpkins on the porch, drinking cider, and eating these donuts."

Cheating on me? My cheeks got a bit hot as I realized I was being a total jealous baking diva here. "They do look good. And there are only a few of those apple muffins left. We could eat these and save those for the kids' breakfast tomorrow."

I looked up and saw the judge watching me, biting back a smile. "I'll return them if you really want. Or I could possibly pick up a second box, just in case they're really good."

I pursed my lips. "Okay. Just in case."

Thankfully, he insisted on paying for everything. I waited while he pulled the SUV up front, and helped him load the entirety of our purchases in the back. Once home, we deposited it all on the front porch, going inside for mugs and plates, as well as newspaper to keep our pumpkin carving mess neatly contained.

"So, what do you have going on this week with the boss and your yoga partner away?" the judge asked as he sawed a jagged-toothed mouth into his pumpkin.

"A pile full of skip traces, a few background checks, and possibly a cheating spouse investigation if the man decides he wants to pursue it. It's always a cheating spouse investigation on the detective side, sadly," I told him as I scooped a warm wet bunch of pumpkin guts out onto the newspaper.

"Daisy made me promise to keep up my daily yoga, but without her here I'm finding myself slacking."

"Slacking? She hasn't even been gone twenty-four hours. At this rate, by the time she gets back you'll be a flabby, weak, inflexible couch potato," he teased.

I looked my jack-o-lantern design over with a critical eye, making a few adjustments with a Sharpie. "Probably. I'm more worried about holding down the fort at work. I only started there seven months ago. J.T.'s never been out of the office before. I'm hoping to be able to handle everything on my own without needing to bother him on vacation. I've never done the bail-bond end of things beyond some risk assessment, though. I'm hoping we don't get any while he's gone because I'm terrified I'll commit us to something I shouldn't."

"Oh, ye of little faith," Judge Beck intoned. "Gator Pierson can hunt down any bail jumper and haul him in. I've seen his videos on YouTube. He's a king among bounty hunters."

I laughed, bending over my pumpkin to saw out a triangle-shaped eye. "The 'Gator' Pierson isn't exactly the man you see on the videos, you know. Although if it came to losing ten grand on a bail jumper, I can completely see him storming into a bad neighborhood and dragging the guy out by his ears. J.T. hates to lose money."

"But he does seem sweet on your friend Daisy."

He *was* sweet on her. Which was completely understandable since I thought Daisy was one of the most amazing women in the world.

"I think she's sweet on him too. She's just scared."

Judge Beck paused mid-carve to shoot me a quizzical glance. "Why? If she likes being with him, enjoys his company, and she's attracted to him, then why be scared? Why hold back?"

"Because it's a huge leap of faith to be emotionally

vulnerable," I told him. "Whether it's because you're not sure if the other party feels the same, or you're worried it's a fleeting emotion on your or their part, or that you're making a mistake and he'll turn out to be a total jerk in six months, letting someone in is scary."

He turned and paid close attention to his jack-o-lantern. "Were you scared to fall in love with Eli?"

"No." I smiled at the memories of Eli and me at college—of all those precious memories I cherished. "Not at all, but I was young and didn't have all that much in the way of experience—good or bad—to make me wary of giving my heart to another. Were you with Heather?"

"I was terrified." He laughed. "Every time I asked a woman out it was like facing a firing squad, but Heather.... We'd been dating six months before I finally worked up the courage to say the 'L' word. Two years before I proposed. I always envied those guys who made it all look so effortless, so easy. But as scared as I was of her saying 'no,' I was more afraid I'd let the opportunity for love pass me by."

I nodded in agreement. "It was just right with Eli, you know? I remember seeing him in classes and thinking he was cute, that he was smart. I remember feeling the pull of attraction. That first date was like puzzle pieces falling into place. It *did* feel easy. He was so honest and up front about his feelings and so was I. It helped that I was positive he was the one, and that I knew he wouldn't hurt me, and that he felt the same about me as I did about him."

J.T. made it clear how he felt about Daisy, just as Eli had with me. And I knew deep down inside he knew Daisy felt the same, she just needed time—time and patience to work through her fears. That's what made me such a fan of this budding relationship between them. His patience, his devotion and understanding...he was a good guy. If Daisy felt any spark at all of attraction toward him, I knew she wouldn't be making a mistake in giving him her heart.

"Do you think you'll ever love again?" Judge Beck asked, still intently focused on his pumpkin.

I thought about the question for a moment. "I really don't know. I mean, I'm open to the idea, but I'm not worried about it. I wouldn't want to feel like I was jumping into something out of loneliness or trying to fill the empty place that Eli's passing left. I've got a job I love. I've got friends. I have some new hobbies. I think it's better if I mourn and settle into life as a single woman before I think about that sort of thing. But if in the future, if the right person comes along, I'd be open to it. I think at my age any relationship is going to be very different from what Eli and I had in our twenties, though. What about you?"

"Definitely." His response was quick and absolute. "I want to make sure I'm not on some rebound romance because of the divorce, or acting out of loneliness or something, and I need to make sure whoever it is loves my kids as much as I do. But I've come to realize that I want someone else in my life. I want to share my time, my emotions, my thoughts, and dreams and future with someone, and I want to share theirs as well. That's just how I'm wired. So yes, I definitely see myself falling in love again. With the right person, of course."

I squirmed, feeling a bit uncomfortable with the direction our conversation had taken. After a few moments of silence, I looked over at the judge's pumpkin, then back at mine, making a very critical comparison.

"Maybe you should have had a career in art instead of law," I told him. "Professional pumpkin carving, or something."

He sat back and eyed his jack-o-lantern with satisfaction. "I loved carving pumpkins when I was a kid. I'd always get the biggest ones I could find and I'd try to think of the scariest face to carve."

"I'll bet you were adorable trick-or-treating. What was your favorite costume?"

He laughed. "My sister always wanted to be a flower, or a princess, or a mouse, or a teapot, so she got the homemade costumes. Mom couldn't figure out how to sew Superman or Batman, so those years I wound up with the dime-store costume-in-a-bag deals. Mom did go all out on the Scooby Doo costume when I was eight, though. And the Godzilla one when I was twelve was pretty cool, although the tail was a lumpy dirty mess by the time I dragged it all through the streets and lawns of our neighborhood."

"A teapot? Your sister seriously dressed up as a teapot one year?"

"Yes, a teapot. I hope you'll get to meet her this year for Christmas. She usually flies in for the holidays. Janet is a hoot. But then again, any girl who wants to be a teapot for Halloween clearly shows comedic genius."

I stood and positioned my jack-o-lantern by the steps, moving the judge's far superior one opposite. "I'll say. That makes my Lassie costume sound so lame."

He chuckled. "Lassie? I'll bet you were adorable."

"Everyone thought I was Bigfoot."

The judge nearly choked on his cider.

"Seriously," I told him. "Mom wasn't the best with a sewing machine. But honestly, it wasn't her fault. There was only one dog costume pattern in the Simplicity catalog, and it was for some kind of felt-type fabric. I insisted on the fur, because Lassie had this luxurious long-haired coat, so Mom used the pattern with reddish brown fur. I really did look like Bigfoot."

"Oh, God." He laughed for a few seconds, then wiped his eyes. "That's hysterical. That's almost as funny as the time

Heather tried to make a flamingo costume for Madison. She was supposed to be a witch, and the night before trick-or-treat, she decided she wanted to be a flamingo. I told her it was too late to change her mind, but Heather ran out the next day and bought pink pants and a pink hooded sweatshirt, then got these feathered angel wings and tried to dye them pink. Madison's flamingo costume consisted of her dressed in pink with wings tied to her arms with yarn and a beak stuck on her face with elastic bands. I've got pictures of it somewhere. Poor thing looked like a flying bottle of Pepto Bismol."

"I'll bet she was the cutest flying bottle of Pepto Bismol ever. Are they going trick-or-treating this year? There aren't many children in the neighborhood, but people drive their kids in from the nearby developments to come around, so we all get candy to hand out."

The last ten years I'd positioned Eli so he could see them from the front window. He'd loved Halloween. We'd had our share of parties and always enjoyed decorating the house for the kids that came by in their costumes. One year he'd even dressed up himself, hiding in a pile of leaves by the porch and jumping up to startle the older children.

"They're a bit old for trick-or-treating," Judge Beck replied.

"No one is too old for trick-or-treating," I scolded. "Let them go if they want. There's plenty of teens that come around. No one minds."

"Henry might," he said. "I'm not sure about Madison, but I'll leave it up to them." He glanced at his watch. "Speaking of which, they should be here soon. I better go throw that pizza in the oven."

"And I better clean up the pumpkin guts." I looked down at the stringy orange mess on top of the newspaper. "Do you all like pumpkin seeds? I can roast them."

He wrinkled his nose. "And pick through all that goop? Isn't it easier to just buy them at the store?"

It was. And the ones at the store never tasted quite as good as the ones made in your own kitchen. I waved him toward the door. "You get going. I'll clean this all up and get the lights in the jack-o-lanterns. And if the kids want pumpkin seeds, I'll make pumpkin seeds."

CHAPTER 9

I was in the dining room, looking for a nice glass bowl to put the roasted pumpkin seeds in when they came out of the oven, when I heard the front door open and the excited voices of two teenagers.

"Kids, you head upstairs," Heather called out. "I need to talk to your father for a moment."

I grimaced, knowing that this was probably going to end up an argument, and here I was stuck in the dining room. Should I make a quick escape to the kitchen, where hopefully thick plaster walls would muffle any loud voices?

No. This was my house. If they wanted a private conversation, they could step outside. I knelt down to grab the bowl I wanted, rattling the glassware so the two in the foyer would know I was here. Over the noise I heard Heather's mumbled words—something about money.

"I'm not paying you alimony," Judge Beck snapped, loud enough for me to clearly hear the words.

"I can't afford to keep the house on the child support alone," Heather snapped back.

I could almost envision the judge's shrug. "Then sell it.

You can buy something cheaper in the same school district. And if you can't, we'll just use my address here to keep the kids in the same schools."

"I don't want to upset them by moving while they're still at home," she insisted. "Put aside that you hate me and don't want to give me a penny more than you have to and think of the children."

"That's a low blow, Heather. Parents move all the time and those children aren't psychologically damaged by a change in houses. I moved here, and Madison and Henry both love this house and the neighborhood. They'll stay in the same school."

"I don't want to move now," she insisted. "And I can't afford the mortgage without alimony."

"Well, maybe you need to get a job."

"I've tried," she retorted. "Do you know what sixteen years of being a stay-at-home-mom does for your resume? Add in the fact that I can't do shift or weekend work and need some flexibility because of the kids' activities, and I'm pretty much looking at making minimum wage."

"You should have thought about that before you asked for a divorce," the judge replied, his voice shaking with anger. "You want the money I bring home. You want the huge fancy home in the rich neighborhood. You want the country club membership. You just don't want me. Well, guess what? You don't get all those other things without me. Sell the house."

I heard Heather choke back a sob. "Madison and Henry already hate me for the divorce. If I sell the house and make them move, they'll hate me even more. Please, Nate. Just five years until Henry goes to college, then I'll sell the house and live in a cardboard box if I have to. I'll agree to let you have the additional equity. I'll even let you take extra out of my portion when we sell. Just please let me keep the house for five years. Please."

It wrenched my heart to hear her beg like that, to figuratively throw herself at her husband's feet. We all liked to have nice things, and Lord knows I didn't relish the idea of losing my home either when I was facing foreclosure after Eli died. I knew in my heart that Heather wasn't being selfish here.

The kids *did* blame her for the divorce. She needed to regain their trust and love and moving wouldn't help that. Neither would her taking so much money from her ex-husband that he couldn't afford to live on his own.

"I wanted to buy my own place," the judge countered softly. "You can't get a loan by yourself on that huge house, and I can't buy anything with my name still on the mortgage. And I can't buy anything with a huge alimony obligation, either. You staying in that house means I don't get to move on and get my own place for five more years. That's hardly fair to me, especially since I'm not even the one who filed for divorce."

I knew what he meant. He did like living here with me, and the kids did too, but it wasn't the same as having his own house where, when the kids were with Heather, he'd feel comfortable bringing a date home to spend the night or feel comfortable wandering around in his underwear. I'd be more than happy to have him stay until Henry went to college. Having the kids live here, heck, having *him* live here, would be like a dream come true. But I wasn't wanting to have a date spend the night or wander around the house in my underwear.

"Okay. I understand." Heather's voice was small and defeated. I heard the rustling sounds of her turning to leave.

"Five years," Judge Beck suddenly announced, as if he were delivering a sentence from the bench. "No alimony, but I will pay the mortgage as well as any repairs on the house for the next five years. You'll get half the profit based on the current appraisal, and I get any extra equity that has built up between now and when you sell it. And you need to list it the moment Henry leaves for college and make every good-faith effort to sell it at that time, or the house transfers to me."

I heard her quick intake of breath even though I was in the dining room. "Thank you, Nate. And I...I'll agree to your revised custody schedule in return."

"Deal." The judge grumbled something under his breath, something that sounded like "Five years. Kay is going to kill me."

Heather laughed. "Hardly. I think she'll be willing to put up with five more years of you."

Put up with? I was ready to jump for joy at the prospect of it.

I heard the front door close and headed out of the dining room, holding the bowl I'd intended for our roasted pumpkin seeds. "I...um, I heard that," I confessed to Judge Beck.

"I know." He sighed. "Kay, I don't want you to think you'll be saddled with me for five years. I told you two, and I'm completely prepared to find something of my own once the divorce is final—an apartment or something."

"You're welcome to stay here for five years or longer if you want. I mean it. This is too big of a house for me to have by myself, and honestly, I need a renter in order to afford the mortgage. We get along. I love your kids. I really don't want to wind up with some weirdo if you move."

He laughed. "I'm glad I rate higher than some weirdo. Honestly though, if you start dating, and my being here is too awkward, just say the word."

I rolled my eyes. "Didn't we have this discussion over pumpkin carving? I'm grieving my husband. And I'm kind of looking forward being a single woman from here on out."

"You say that now, but in a few years, you might change

your mind. Just let me know and I'll move. I don't want to hold you back."

"Likewise." Before he could reply, I turned around and headed into the kitchen.

I'd just taken the pumpkin seeds out of the oven to cool when Madison came in and plopped down at the kitchen island. "Is that your dinner? We ate at Mom's, but can I help?"

"I'm not having pumpkin seeds for dinner," I teased. "But I *am* getting ready to make espresso chip scones and double chocolate muffins if you want to help with that."

Madison jumped up from her chair and started pulling the ingredients out of the cabinets. I loved how she'd gotten to know my favorite recipes, and was always willing to help out.

Which reminded me....

"As soon as you're done mixing up the scones, take a look at that recipe book on the table. I got it from one of the auction baskets at the golf tourney. There's a short rib recipe in there that looks pretty good."

"Can I make it for dinner one night this week?" she asked. "Ooh, but the dishwasher is still broken, isn't it? I hate to cook anything that's going to be too hard to clean up."

I felt a stab of guilt over the dishwasher. "Yes, it's still broken, but I don't think this recipe is going to dirty any more dishes than hamburgers or Crock Pot chicken. Plus, we'll clean as we go so there won't be such a mess after dinner."

Madison fired up the espresso maker and started in on her dough while I began melting chocolate for the muffins. "How about I make the short ribs on Wednesday? I can ask Dad to swing by the store on the way home from school for the meat and anything else we need."

"I have a viewing Wednesday night for Olive's uncle, so

maybe Thursday? Unless you and Henry plan on trick-or-treating."

"Olive's uncle died?" Madison exclaimed. "I'm so sorry to hear that. Thursday will work, though. We don't have practice that night, and I'm not going out. Maybe we can eat a bit later so I can help hand out candy? And that way if Henry goes trick-or-treating, he'll be back in time for dinner?"

"Good idea." She was such a mature, thoughtful girl. I glanced over at Eli's ghost in his usual spot over by the basement steps and wondered if we would have done as good a job of parenting as Judge Beck and Heather. Both Madison and Henry were smart, kind, and such a joy to be around.

By the time we had the muffins and scones in the oven, my imagination conjured up a daughter and a son just like Madison and Henry, only Eli's and my children would have been about fifteen years older. Actually, I would have had grandkids to spoil at this point, little babies to love on, to visit me for weekends.

But fate had other plans for Eli and me. My hope now was that Madison and Henry remained in touch as they grew, and that it would be their children I'd be spoiling in my older years.

Madison and I sat down to look at the recipe book, and especially the Kentucky short rib recipe. It looked fairly straight forward. The short ribs were boiled, then coated with the sauce and roasted in the oven to finish. The sauce was a combination of lemon juice, cider vinegar, Worcestershire sauce, ketchup, chili sauce, dry mustard, and brown sugar. We discussed the recipe, decided we'd only need a nice salad to go along with the short ribs, then wrote down the things she'd need to buy. We took the muffins and scones out of the oven and put them somewhere safe to cool where Taco wouldn't eat them all, then Madison put some of the roasted pumpkin seeds in a bowl and went upstairs to where her dad was playing a video game with Henry.

I made myself a sandwich, let Taco inside and fed him his dinner, then headed into the parlor to do some knitting. Eli's ghost followed me in, as always, but as I sat down on the couch, I noticed the second ghost forming on the opposite side of the room.

The woman's ghost. I noticed she vanished whenever someone else was in the room, only showing herself when I was alone, but she didn't seem to mind Eli's spirit. She kept her distance, but the two ghosts were in the same room with me and Taco.

Taco glared at the woman's ghost, sneezed, then left the room. The cat tolerated Eli's spirit, but made it plain he wanted nothing to do with any other apparition.

"I don't know what I can do to help you," I told the ghost who wasn't my husband. "I'll do what I can, but it's going to be up to the police to find your murderer."

Who was I kidding? I continued working on the scarf, the two ghosts like sentinels at opposite ends of the room. I would help her, not because she was hanging out in my house, but because it's what I did. A woman had been killed, her body hidden in the grave of a friend's cousin. And that meant I'd do all I could to help bring the murderer to justice —for Olive, for DeLanie, and for this woman whose ghost hovered at the far end of my parlor.

CHAPTER 10

J was up to my neck in skip traces as well as some research on a potential insurance fraud issue when Miles popped into the office. His eyes immediately went to the basket of muffins and scones over by the coffee machine.

"Yes, they're for you." I laughed. "Go ahead and help yourself. J.T. is out of town this week, and I'm hardly going to eat all of those myself."

"Heard you had some excitement after the golf tournament." He grabbed two scones, then stuffed a muffin in his mouth, taking a huge bite and talking as he chewed. "I'm jealous."

I waved at the muffin. "So, are you going to give me some information in return for my feeding you? The paper this morning didn't have anything additional. All I know is that the body was female and apparently she was shot."

He crammed the rest of the muffin in his mouth. "You didn't hear this from me, but twenty-five-year-old white female. Cause of death at first look was gunshot wound to the chest. Bled out from what the responding guys are guessing. M.E. will do an autopsy and send away for labs, but from what the officers said it was pretty straightforward."

I shook my head, sick that a twenty-five-year-old woman was dead. Shot. Thrown into someone else's grave.

"Her name was Mary Allen," he added.

"You already identified her?" I watched him chow down on one of the scones. "Did she have her license in her pocket or something?"

"Weirdly enough, yeah. Wallet with her license, twenty bucks, and an ATM card. We ran her prints just to make sure and she was in the system."

I frowned, and not just because Miles was talking with his mouth full. "In the system? She'd been arrested at one time?"

"Arrested, charged, convicted, and served time. Although served time is a bit of an exaggeration. Possession. First offense. She did work release for six months and got two years' probation."

"Possession?" I stared at the deputy. "Drugs? Prescription drugs? Like Oxy?"

He nodded. "She was eighteen at the time. Clean since then from our records, but given that she was shot and dumped in an open grave, we're thinking maybe she'd relapsed."

"And maybe there was a connection between her and David Driver," I mused.

"Who?" The word was barely intelligible. I glared at Miles but he swallowed, shot me a grin, and grabbed another muffin.

"David Driver. That's whose grave she was dumped in."

He shrugged. "Maybe. Maybe not. It could have just been an opportune place to hide the body. And no one would have ever been the wiser if they hadn't been relocating that casket. Weird, huh?"

More than weird.

"Didn't someone report Mary Allen missing? How could she just vanish and no one know about it?"

"Evidently her parents had moved out of state years ago while she stayed here. They did fill out a missing person's report back in May, but a twenty-five-year-old woman with a history of drug use goes missing, we tend to assume the worst."

"David Driver was buried six months ago," I mused. "She had to have been killed then."

"Yep." He wrapped two muffins in a coffee filter and stuck them in his pocket. "And I'm doubting someone killed her and kept her body sitting around until a handy funeral, so we're assuming she was killed on that day."

"So, what's next?" I eyed the skip traces and insurance fraud files and knew they were about to wait.

"We interview her friends and family and try to find out what was happening in her life, who might have wanted her dead, if she was still on drugs or clean, if there was anything else going on that might point to who would kill her."

"Keep me up to date?" I asked as Miles headed toward the door.

"Keep my belly filled with your baked goods and I'll be happy to share anything nonconfidential with you." He eyed the half-empty basket. "Lemon zest pound cake, and I might even share the confidential stuff with you."

I laughed and waved him out the door, then helped myself to what was left of the muffins. I so wanted to go over to the cemetery, to meet with Melanie and try to figure out how a murder victim had come to be buried in with David Driver. I'd felt like I owed it to Olive and to DeLanie to find out the why, but now I was having second thoughts.

It wasn't my business. They hadn't asked me to look into this, and I was beginning to think it was more morbid curiosity on my part than the need to help them. Maybe it *was* just a coincidence. Maybe David Driver's grave was just a convenient spot to dump a body. I had work here to do, especially with J.T. gone for the week. The police were on this case. I needed to do my work and not go running off investigating something that might have nothing to do with DeLanie Driver's son.

So, I spent the rest of the morning doing skip traces, and when lunch time came, I bundled up and drove into Milford to check out that used appliance store Suzette had told me about.

Berton's Used Appliances was in the industrial side of town, across the street from the feed store and just down the street from the milk processing center. I had to cross over a set of railroad tracks and drive down a pothole-filled gravel lane to get to their parking lot. The building looked like it hadn't been touched in the last fifty years. Cement block walls were thick with untold layers of yellowish paint. The glass entryway door had a metal grate bolted onto the frame and the linoleum on the floor was chipped and gouged. There were appliances lined up in three neat rows, organized by type. Closest to the door were stoves, and the ones I saw were most definitely the no-frills sort with actual knobs to turn the coil burners on and off, and little signs taped to the front to indicate whether they were self-cleaning or not.

A woman approached me from back behind a row of refrigerators. She was sporting a perm the likes of which I hadn't seen since the eighties.

"I'm looking for a dishwasher," I told her with a tentative smile.

She grinned. "The mechanical kind, I'm assuming. Otherwise you should go two blocks down to the temp service. They've probably got a two-for-one on dishwashers, but you don't gotta pay ours overtime."

I forced out a polite laugh. "The mechanical kind. My budget is around two hundred. Oh, and do you deliver them? And install them?"

She nodded. "That's an extra fifty, unless you need plumbing work done too."

I did some quick math in regards to my meager savings account. "It's replacing an existing dishwasher, so I don't think there's any special plumbing needed beyond what you'd usually do to swap out a broken appliance with one that works."

She pursed her lips and inclined her head. "Well then, come on over here with me and take a look at what we've got in your price range."

I followed her over to a grouping of four virtually indistinguishable dishwashers. They were all white. They all had buttons with the symbols or text worn nearly off them. They all had a variety of dents and a few rust spots. I swallowed hard, thinking of how Eli and I had bought top of the line appliances, carefully selecting them for features and appearance. Of course, that top of the line dishwasher was now broken, where these dated, dented ones worked.

"How are they on energy efficiency?" I asked.

The woman looked at me as if I were insane. "They all work. We give you a sixty-day warranty and the option to purchase a service plan. I don't know anything about energy efficiency."

I opened one up, eyeing the racks. Clearly, they weren't customizable. Would half my dishes even fit in here without being able to fold part of the rack down or remove the baskets? I felt like such a snob turning my nose up at the lack of features. They worked. And they were in my price range. I didn't have six hundred dollars or more to buy something with all the bells and whistles, and unless the dishwasher fairy was going to visit my house in the night and leave me a stack of money, I wasn't going to come up with the cash in the next two weeks. It was either this, or confess to the judge and the kids that I didn't have the money to replace the broken appliance. And wouldn't for a few months at a minimum.

That would be mortifying. But having someone install a dented, rusty replacement was just as mortifying. Either way I was going to need to swallow my pride and make a decision.

I looked up to see the woman eyeing me with a bit of sympathy as if she could sense my dilemma.

"We did get another one in yesterday that's not on the floor yet," she told me. "One of the contractors sold it to us for wholesale. It was a custom order that didn't get picked up. I could let you have it for three hundred with the installation thrown in."

That was pushing my budget a bit, but I was willing to take a look at it, so I stood and followed her back into a cement floor storage room full of parts and dismantled appliances. It reminded me a lot of Mr. Peter's house before his nephew had begun cleaning it out.

"This is it." The woman stopped and gestured Vanna White style to a gleaming dishwasher, so new it still had the energy efficient sticker on the door. It automatically adjusted water and energy based on the load. It had a special top-rack zone jet system. It had independent rotating spray arms. It had a smart dry feature. It had a sanitizing wash setting, a zone booster, customizable racks. It was amazing.

It was bordello red.

I was in college in the seventies. I remembered how everyone's houses were lined with wood paneling, that the main three colors for appliances were harvest gold, avocado, and copper. I'll even admit that I had a sort of fond nostalgia for that era in home design—not that I wanted to replicate it in my current house, but still a fond nostalgia. But beyond that, I was a neutral-tone, stainless steel kind of gal. That I could have lived with. The current, nonfunctional dishwasher was one of those hideously expensive ones where the front was made to match the cabinetry, hiding all the modern appliances out of sight behind a lovely wood finish. I knew I couldn't afford that. I knew I couldn't afford stainless steel. I'd reconciled myself to the fact that I'd end up with a plain, white, non-matching dishwasher. I'd almost reconciled myself to one of the dented, slightly rusted, absolutely featureless dishwashers out in the showroom. But this lipstick-bright red?

"Awful, isn't it?" The woman made one of those snort-laughs. "I'll bet the customers were drunk off their whatoozies, and when this thing came in they had a major case of the regrets. Nice dishwasher though. These things go for eight, nine hundred bucks. Course, no one wants a red dishwasher. And most of our customers are putting appliances in rental places and investment properties. They don't want something with all these electronic thingamajigs to go wrong. Basic stuff that's hard for tenants to break and cheap to fix or replace. That's what moves the most here. Still, thought you might want to take a look at it since it seems you wanted something a bit more than what we usually carry."

These were my choices. Tell everyone we'd be dishwasher-less for a few months until I saved up the money. Buy a rust-and-dent base model from the showroom and have a bit left in change. Or spend my whole savings account on this red monstrosity that had all the features I could ever dream of and would look like an appliance murder in the middle of my kitchen.

"Can I think on it and let you know by the end of the week?" I asked the woman.

She laughed. "Honey, this thing ain't going nowhere. And if you want one of the white ones out there in the showroom, we've got plenty. If you let me know by the end of the week, I can probably get Rodney to swing by first thing Monday and install it for you—if you're local, that is."

"Locust Point," I told her.

"Oh yeah. Rodney can totally get to you early Monday if you like." She fished a bent card out of her pocket and handed it to me. "Just call and let me know."

I stuck the card in my purse and headed back to the office and my pile of skip traces, weighing the pros and cons of each option. How hard would it be to paint an appliance? Could I maybe glue something over the red? It would be awesome to have a dishwasher with that top-rack zone jet system and independent rotating spray arms. And the sanitize feature…

Red. I winced and wished that four hundred dollars would fall out of the sky and make this decision so much easier.

* * *

I ENDED up leaving work a bit early to swing by the cemetery, because I was nosy, and I knew there was a ghost waiting home at my house that needed me to help solve her murder. The canopy and police tape were still up around David's grave, as was the cluster of ghosts, so I kept going and parked by the offices. Melanie was inside, surrounded by paperwork. She looked up with her usual calm, cool smile, but I could see the tightness around her mouth and the dark circles under her eyes that her concealer was doing little to mask.

"Mrs. Carrera. How can I help you?"

I quickly decided to be as straightforward as possible, but

to phrase this as a concerned owner of my husband's grave plot.

"I've been thinking about what happened Saturday," I started out.

She nodded. "I'm sure all of us have. It was quite a shock. I can assure you that is not something that has ever happened here before."

"How could you know that, though? It's not like you exhume bodies all the time. There could be murder victims hidden in other graves. Maybe there's someone who has discovered this is the perfect place to dispose of his serial-killer victims. This sort of thing could have been going on for years, some crazy murderer putting his victims in other people's graves."

Melanie's left eye twitched, her smile becoming stiff. "I sincerely doubt there is some sort of crime ring using our cemetery to hide bodies, Mrs. Carrera."

"How could someone, an employee of yours, manage to fill in a grave plot without noticing a tarp-wrapped body in there? Someone probably paid him to look the other way. And if they paid him to look the other way once, they most likely paid him to do it dozens of times. Several friends and I were discussing having you open our loved ones' graves to check."

She paled. I was sure she was calculating the cost of having to open hundreds of graves, then refill them and lay down fresh sod. And of course, after what had happened, people would insist the cemetery needed to do this at their own cost, since they were clearly negligent in allowing such a horrible mistake to happen to David Driver's grave.

"I can assure you that your husband's grave has not been violated in such a way, Mrs. Carrera. Please tell your friends that there is no need to worry. There is no need to go about disturbing their loved ones' eternal rest in this fashion."

"But if it happened with David Driver's grave, what guarantee do we have that it hasn't happened to others?"

"This was a terrible one-time occurrence, and we're taking precautions to make sure it doesn't happen again."

"What sort of precautions?" I tried to look panicked, as though I thought there were murder victims double stacked in all the graves out there.

"We've fired our current excavation crew and are in the process of replacing them."

"But if you have a bad employee looking the other way about this sort of thing, then firing him won't change the past," I argued.

"It wasn't an employee," Melanie said, clearly deciding to throw someone else under the bus. "We don't like people to know it because we pride ourselves on being a family operation, but we contract out the excavation work. It takes two to three people, and it didn't make sense to have them on the payroll full time so six months ago we started using a contractor. We'll be bringing this function back in house so this sort of thing won't happen again. And I can assure you that this was truly a one-time issue. We weren't even using this contractor when your husband was buried."

I nodded, trying to look relieved. "Oh, good. Now I can tell DeLanie Driver that she doesn't have to sue you. She can sue this contractor instead. Do you have their name?"

Melanie got even whiter and fumbled in her desk drawer, pulling out an invoice and copying the name, address, and phone number from it to a sticky note with shaky hands.

"Here." She thrust the sticky note to me. "Give this to her. This is the contractor we were using."

As I left the office, I looked down at the note and wondered if I had time to pay Baughman's Excavating a visit.

CHAPTER 11

*B*aughman Excavating was a small operation. Their offices were in the industrial section of town in what looked like a strip mall for companies that dealt in the trades. There was the company name in black stenciling on a primer-gray steel door. I opened it to find a six-by-eight office barely big enough for an old metal desk and two chairs. A blonde bearded man in his thirties looked up at me and shut the filing cabinet he'd been rifling through.

"Can I help you?" He looked rather frazzled, his hair oddly spiked as if he'd spent the last few hours pulling on it.

"Are you Bob Baughman?" At his nod I continued. "I was at the cemetery Saturday for the relocation of the Driver remains and I was wondering if you could answer a few questions about your contract work with Windy Oaks."

He reached up with one hand and jerked his fingers through his hair, causing it to stand even more on end. "You the police? A lawyer? Is she gonna sue us? I've spent all morning looking for the paperwork for that job and haven't had time to get a lawyer yet, so maybe you could come back?"

"I'm not the police or a lawyer," I assured him. "I work for Pierson Investigation and Recovery Services, but I'm not here on any official capacity. I'm just trying to find out what happened."

"You and me both, lady," he grumbled. "This is gonna ruin me. I'm not a big business. It's just me and my brother running things here and my nephew Jake when we need a hand. We don't have any big equipment, just the little digger and a few attachments. Outside of the cemetery, most of our work is running utility lines in new home construction or trenching for drainage pipes. Now we just lost the cemetery contract." He shook his head. "Word gets around that lady at Windy Oaks is blaming us, we might find ourselves out of business."

I wanted to feel sorry for the guy, but they had buried a murder victim in a grave. Either they were blind, or they knew what was going on and took the chance no one would ever find out. But before I could mention it, something else hit me.

"You said it's just you and your brother and nephew? There were three men there Saturday, and you weren't one of them."

"We didn't get a call to do that relocation on Saturday." He scowled. "I read about it in the paper and wondered about that. Guess they were using someone else for Saturday, which ticks me off since that would have been the weekend rate for us. We were supposed to have an exclusive contract with Windy Oaks. That's why we gave them such a good price."

"Would they have used in-house staff maybe?" I asked. "The cemetery manager did mention they were a family business."

"Right," he scoffed. "Family meaning the owners. Most of their staff isn't related, although that woman in charge of it all is some sort of niece of something. They've got their own equipment, mainly mowers and stuff, but they probably have a bucket attachment for one of the tractors. Their landscaping guys could have been doing that Saturday job for them, although they should have called us. We had a contract."

"It was probably last minute," I told him. "There's a chance they didn't even know until a few hours before."

"Still shoulda called us," he groused. "It's our contract. Saturday afternoon? I'd have dropped everything for a few hundred bucks on a Saturday afternoon."

Few hundred? I knew they charged over a thousand to open the grave for Eli's remains. What kind of profit were these cemetery people making? Although I probably shouldn't be getting sidetracked by that sort of thing.

"You did open and close the Driver grave when he was buried six months ago, though?" I asked.

He looked down at the folder in his hand. "I'm not the best at keeping records, but I found it. If I've got a file on it, it means we did the job."

"The three of you were there? And didn't notice a body wrapped in a tarp in the grave? You didn't see anything?"

Bob opened the file. "We all take turns. The job really only takes two people—one to run the excavator and the other to shovel and make sure everything is where it needs to be and that we're not knocking over headstones or making a mess. Most funerals are on Friday evening, or on the weekend, so we're real busy Thursday through Sunday night. Mornings we go in early, before the gates open, and dig the graves for that day. The cemetery staff comes by after and puts up the canopies, the casket stand and drapes, and the chairs and stuff. Oh, and they put a drape over the dirt so nobody can see it and everything looks all nice. Then at night, once the gates close at dusk, we come back and fill in."

"The casket's already lowered by then?" I asked.

He nodded. "They lower the casket right after the mourners leave, but keep the canopy and the stand there until the gates close, partly for safety and partly to look nice and respectful for people coming and going. At dusk, they take down the canopies and the casket stand and haul everything away—drapes and chairs and all. By the time we come in, it's just the box that holds the dirt and the hole in the ground. When we're done, we haul the dirt boxes over to the supply shed before we leave. The next morning, the landscaping guys put down sod and the caretaker has someone put the little metal marker on the grave, to mark the spot until the granite marker gets made."

"And the gates are locked when you get there? You have a key or something?"

He nodded. "The gates are always locked. It's a pain in the butt. I'm hauling a trailer with the digger and I've got to get out, unlock the gates, pull through, then lock them back up. And do it again when we leave."

"And you've never found them unlocked when you get there?" I prodded.

He shook his head. "The cemetery is real careful about that. They don't want vandals or anyone messing with the graves at night. There's someone who spends the night in that house up front, but I don't think he patrols the grounds or anything. I know sometimes people stay too late and get locked in and have to knock on the door and have the guy let them out. That's how strict they are about when they lock and open the gates."

"Anyone else have keys that you're aware of?"

"No, but I'm sure there's lawn crews and former employees that might have them. It's not exactly a high-security system there and I doubt they've changed the locks in the last five years or so."

"Is there anything you remember about that night David Driver was buried? Were you one of the people there, or was it your brother and nephew?"

"You sure you're not a cop?" he asked in an accusing voice. Then he sighed and looked through the papers in the folder. "Invoice was for two of us. I signed off on it, so I must have been there. Probably me and Junior from what we charged, which means I would have been running the digger and Junior with the shovel."

I imagined this Junior taking a payoff and not letting his uncle know that there was a body in the open grave, but that didn't seem all that smart. There was too much chance that his uncle would have glanced down and saw what was going on. Either they were both in on it, or neither was.

"How dark is it? Would either of you have been able to see a body wrapped in a tarp in the grave?" I found it hard to believe this man before me had knowingly buried Mary Allen's body in that grave, but how could he have *not* known?

"Gates close at dusk and we end up rolling in usually a bit after. Depending on how many graves we had that night and the order we did them in, it could have been full dark by the time we filled that one in. Don't know if there was a moon or not, but the digger has a lamp and we wear lights on our heads. I would have been running the machine, but Junior would have been checking to make sure everything was going okay. He would have noticed if there was a tarp down in the grave and let me know. Heck, *I* would have noticed. We would have probably thought something fell down there when they were taking down the canopy or something and ended up calling the manager. We would have noticed."

This was so frustrating. I couldn't imagine another person brought excavating equipment in through locked gates to re-dig the grave, put Mary Allen in there, and fill it back in. It would have taken too long to do that by hand with shovels, in spite of what the horror movies always showed, but what other option was there?

Unless…Hadn't Bob said the cemetery had a tractor with a bucket? Maybe one of their employees with a key snuck in at night while the guy living there slept and put Mary Allen in that grave. Maybe Melanie had thrown these guys under the bus because she didn't want one of her own employees arrested for improper disposal of remains and aiding and abetting a murderer.

"You know…" Bob's eyes focused off into the distance as he closed the folder. "A tarp in the grave would have caught our eye, but we wouldn't have thought twice if the plot was already half full."

"Pardon? Half full of what?"

"Dirt." He turned and slid the folder back into the filing cabinet. "A few of these services, people come up afterward and throw some dirt into the grave. It's a custom with some people. Makes it all final somehow."

"A few handfuls of dirt aren't going to cover up a body in a bright blue tarp," I argued. "And besides, if you and your nephew would have noticed a tarp in the grave, I'm pretty sure mourners in broad daylight would have, especially if they just lowered the casket down and someone tossed a body on top."

"People don't always throw handfuls, they each sometimes toss in a shovelful of dirt. You get a lot of mourners, and that can mean the grave is half full before we even get there. I'm not saying that's what happened. I'm saying that if we showed up to fill in a grave and it was already half full, we wouldn't have thought anything was wrong. We don't know what sort of funeral people are having. We just dig the holes and fill them in."

I resisted the urge to grab Bob and hug him. "So, the casket gets lowered, and sometime between the end of the service and you all showing up, someone tosses a body into the grave and shovels a bunch of dirt on top of it."

He nodded. "Could have happened. And I'll be honest, lady, it wouldn't be all that hard to do. The canopy always has one side up for privacy, sometimes all three sides in bad weather. Just pull up like you're paying respects to someone, make sure no one is around and quickly take the body from your car to the grave plot. Then just shovel in some dirt and leave."

"Which means it could have been anyone," I said.

"Yep. Could have been anyone. But definitely wasn't me, my brother, or my nephew."

CHAPTER 12

$\mathcal{I}$ was later than usual getting home due to my detour, but I still beat the rest of my household. After school sports practice bought Judge Beck some extra precious time in his office, allowing him to pick the kids up at five instead of three-thirty. I raced in my door at six, threw my bag on the couch and got down to the most important activity of the evening—feeding my cat.

Taco was waiting by the door, loudly informing me that he didn't appreciate the delay in his dinner schedule. It was a testament to how food-centric the cat was that he didn't try to squeeze past me to run outside the moment I opened the door. I usually let him have some outside time right when I got home, knowing he'd be yowling to be let in and fed promptly at quarter to six. I'd been determined this summer to make Taco a house cat, worried that his wandering was going to end up with him flattened by a car or eaten by one of the neighborhood dogs that he liked to torment. My cat was a master of manipulation by guilt, though. Not even the fancy enclosed cat run that Henry and Madison had helped me build eased the remorse I felt at my poor cat's confinement.

So Taco once more had his free time, although I tried to orchestrate his forays into the great outdoors so that he'd be especially motivated to return home at a certain time.

Dinner was clearly more important than chasing birds or tormenting the neighbor's dog. I somehow managed to make it to the kitchen without tripping over Taco and promptly filled his bowl full of Happy Cat kibble. Then I threw some noodles on to boil and checked the Crock Pot beef stroganoff that had been simmering away since this morning. I was just draining the noodles when I head the front door.

"We're home!" Henry shouted. "And Taco snuck out!"

Drat.

"I'll get him," Madison called. If that cat was going to come for anyone, it was Madison. I think she'd been secretly slipping him treats, because Taco adored her.

Henry set the table, and by the time Madison returned with my cat, dinner was ready. We ate, and while the kids did the dishes, Judge Beck and I began our nightly ritual of spreading our work out on the newly cleaned dining room table. Sometimes the kids sat at either end doing their homework as we caught up on what didn't quite get done during the hours of nine-to-five, and sometimes the kids took their work upstairs and left us to our laptops and files. As much as I loved Madison and Henry's company, I was kind of glad they went upstairs this evening because I was dying to tell the judge all I'd found out about the body in David Driver's grave, and these weren't the sort of details I felt young ears should be hearing.

When I finished, Judge Beck looked like he wasn't pleased to have been hearing these details, either.

"The police are investigating it, right?" he asked me. "It's a murder. They've assigned a detective and are investigating."

I knew where he was going with this. "Yes, they're investigating. Miles said they'd probably start by looking into this woman's background and questioning her friends and family."

"Then let them investigate, Kay. This isn't a case you're doing for work. I know you're smack in the middle of it, as you always seem to be, but it's not your case. Just let the police do their job and don't dig around on your own. Not on this one."

I was a bit stung. I'd thought he would have been intrigued, just as interested in finding out how Mary Allen's body had ended up in that grave as I was. He'd definitely expressed concerns before, but not like this.

"I dig around. It's what I do. Before I had this job, I was an investigative journalist. So, I've made a career out of digging around. And may I remind you that in the past seven months, my digging around has often turned up information that has helped the police to find and bring a killer to justice."

"This is different." He pushed aside a stack of files and leaned toward me, lowering his voice. "Kay, I've seen what these people do when they feel threatened. This woman in the grave, you said she had a drug conviction in her past? I've seen this sort of thing before—many, many times before. These drug gangs are violent and dangerous, and if they know you're digging around, they won't hesitate to do the same to you that they did to this woman."

I shivered at his insinuation. "But we don't know it's drug related. No one knows that. For all we know, she hasn't crossed that line since her arrest seven years ago."

His eyes met mine and held them. "Gunshot to the chest. Body dumped in an open grave and covered up. Either no one saw anything, or everyone is afraid to say a word. Kay, it was a drug hit. Please don't involve yourself in this. Please."

When he put it that way, I felt a whole lot less offended by his comments—and a whole lot more afraid.

I sighed. "Okay. I mean, I'll try. I can't promise anything because sometimes I end up in the middle of things, like you said, and I'm not going to just walk away if that happens. But I won't go facing down gangsters or anything."

The judge made a harrumph noise, then pulled his files over to him. I hid a smile, knowing he was just worried—and that he knew full well I had no intention of letting this go. I was too curious, too nosy.

But I really didn't want to end up shot by a drug gang. No, that would not be fun.

The doorbell rang. I heard a stampede of feet coming down the stairs and didn't bother to get up, figuring it was one of Madison or Henry's friends coming over to help with homework.

"Miss Kay!" Henry's voice called out. "It's Miss Olive to see you!"

I got up, wondering if maybe DeLanie had forgotten something when she'd spent the night, although the woman had my number. I'd assumed she would have called me herself. Olive was inside, unwinding a long scarf from around her neck. Henry headed back upstairs and I motioned my friend in, offering her a cup of coffee or something else to drink.

"Oh, no. No, thank you. I won't be long. I was just down at Suzette's for dinner and wanted to stop by and ask you something," she said with an apologetic smile.

The pair of us sat in my parlor. Olive took a deep breath and smoothed her palms along her pants. "I want to hire you."

I blinked. "Hire me to do what?"

"Investigate. I want to hire you to investigate what happened in David's grave."

Oh, my. Judge Beck wasn't going to be happy about this one, but at least I now had a legitimate business reason for my nosy inquiries.

"I know I could have stopped by your office tomorrow and made it all official," she continued, "but I was right down the street and this way, I don't have to run in from Milford in the middle of the day."

I was too embarrassed to tell her that I'd already been investigating, so I busied myself grabbing a pad of paper and a pencil, supposedly to take notes. "The police are on the case, you know. I don't want to turn a potential client away, especially one that's a friend, but I don't want you to waste your money."

"The police are investigating that woman's murder, the one in the grave. I want you to find out who put her in there and why. I want to know if there's some connection between her and David, if there's a reason his grave was chosen."

Yes, exactly what I'd already been trying to dig up. J.T. would be thrilled that I'd actually be getting paid for my snooping for once.

"That's going to come out in the police investigation, though," I pointed out, just to be transparent.

"The police are only going to release certain details. They're going to be working on building a murder case against someone. I want to know more than that, things that they might not bother with because it doesn't tie in neatly to their case. I want to know why. I have a sick feeling that David's grave wasn't just a convenient spot, that this woman's death had something to do with his."

Suddenly I understood her. "You're wondering if David's overdose wasn't accidental?"

She nodded. "I know it sounds crazy. From what the papers say, this woman was shot, but I keep thinking about David. DeLanie doesn't like to talk about it because she thinks we judge her and him for his addiction, but we were very empathetic. Everyone battles demons, and David was family. I know Dad and Uncle Ford were helping David out, making sure he got into a better rehab than DeLanie could have afforded on her own. This last time, Uncle Ford paid for the whole inpatient stay. Dad let that slip one night after the funeral. Uncle Ford didn't want anyone to know. This last time…we thought he'd had it beat. He got a job at Uncle Ford's company. He'd been going to his meetings. He got out of rehab around Christmas and everything seemed to change for him. We all saw it. The last few months before he died, he seemed happy. Happier than I'd ever seen him. When he died, I couldn't believe it. No one could believe it."

"Sometimes people are really good at covering up their struggles," I told her. "Sometimes it only takes one little thing to tip them over the edge."

"I know." Olive reached up and wiped under her eyes. "I know, and that's why we all kept quiet. I'm sure the family of every overdose victim thinks briefly that it's foul play, that their loved one was clean until the end. Our society sees addiction as a symptom of a weak personality, of a failure. No one wants their son to carry that legacy with them after death."

I leaned forward. "Are you sure you want me to do this, Olive? The only thing I might uncover is a lot of hurt. Sometimes it's better to live with the memories you have of someone than find out what you hoped for was a lie."

"I want to hire you." Her gaze met mine. "I want to know how and why that woman's body ended up in David's grave. And if that means I find out David was doing drugs the moment he got back from rehab, that he was stealing or dealing, or doing something horrible, then so be it. My only request is that if you find out anything bad about David, you only tell me. DeLanie has been through enough. She never married. David's father was some casual boyfriend that took off on her when she got pregnant. His name's not even on David's birth certificate. David was all she had."

I picked up that pad of paper and pencil once more, went over our fee structure, then at Olive's nod, I got to work. Starting with a confession.

"I'm about to save you a lot of money. Completely free of charge, I've already spoken to a deputy, the manager at the cemetery, and the contractor that does the gravedigging work for them."

Olive blinked, then laughed. "Seriously? I should have known. Why am I even paying you? You were going to investigate this anyway, weren't you?"

"Yes, but the difference is that since I have a paying client, I have an excuse to use my worktime to check all this out without my boss firing me."

She smirked. "Isn't he following Daisy around like a love-sick puppy dog? Your best friend? Girl, he's not going to fire you. That man knows his chances of getting Daisy in bed drop to a big fat zero if he fires her best friend."

"Probably true, but I'm not about to press my luck. Now, a few questions, if you don't mind, Ms. Johnson. About David's interment, did part of the graveside service involve friends and family putting a handful, or a shovelful of dirt into the grave?"

She winced. "No. I know some people do that, but not us. We didn't even want them to lower the casket until after we left. It seemed so final, you know? We were all so raw. So shocked over David's death."

"Who was there at the service? Anyone you didn't know?"

"A lot of people I didn't know. Lots of David's friends, some I think from his recovery group. There were some people that worked with him at Uncle Ford's and some from other jobs. DeLanie has the guestbook people signed at the funeral. Do you want me to get that?"

"I'll go over and see her tomorrow. Do you remember who was there from the cemetery? Their staff?"

Olive frowned a moment, then shook her head. "I remember people from the funeral home, but not specifically who. Our minister from the church giving the service. That Melanie woman from the cemetery was off to the side talking to the man from the funeral parlor, I remember. They were so respectful, so helpful to DeLanie and us all. Very discrete. I think there might have been a few men who looked like they were there to lower the casket after we left, but they held back. They didn't have suits on, just work clothes, so I'm sure they were part of the cemetery staff."

"Can you describe them at all?"

"I didn't pay much attention to them, just saw them sorta out of the corner of my eye as we were getting settled. I probably wouldn't have noticed them at all, but I was looking for Aunt Sarah and Uncle Ford and making sure they were seated up front by DeLanie and saw them. They were white. Men. Adult, but not old, so maybe in their thirties or forties? I'm not really sure."

"Do you recognize the name Mary Allen?" I'd assumed the police had notified her next of kin already and released that information to the public, but just in case I was keeping it vague. I didn't want to get Miles in trouble for blabbing things he shouldn't.

"No." Olive shook her head. "But I didn't know any of David's friends outside of high school. We were close when we were kids, but after I went away to college, we grew apart. I'd sometimes see him during the holidays—even with the feud between Aunt Sarah and DeLanie, Uncle Ford always made sure she and David came over for the big Christmas Eve dinner. We didn't really run in the same social circles, though. And David had other interests, so even when we were kids we didn't see each other much outside of family get togethers."

"Do you think DeLanie would know? Were they close enough that she would have met most of his friends?"

"They were close, but I doubt my mother knows all my friends." She chuckled. "Heck, she probably doesn't know who I'm dating half the time. And if this Mary Allen was one of David's friends from when he was using, then I'll bet he took pains to keep her from DeLanie. The boy wasn't dumb. Not like he's going to introduce his mother to his dealer or anything."

I hesitated, not sure how to bring this up, especially since right at the moment there were no shadowy forms at the edge of my vision. "Do you...do you sense any ghosts in my house right now?"

Olive got that faraway expression on her face, her gaze focusing off into the distance. "A man. Early sixties. He's the one who is always here whenever I come. I don't think he strays far from the house."

"But no one else?"

Her eyes met mine. "No. Why? Has the dead woman's ghost contacted you?"

"I think it's her. She's just lurking, and she only appears when I'm alone."

Olive shook her head. "Then I'm afraid I can't help. I could try to summon her, but if she's that reticent, I'd probably fail."

I nodded, wondering if I could somehow talk the ghost into sticking around so Olive could ask her who had killed her and why. But while some ghosts, like Holt's, were chatty, others only repeated obscure phrases, and some didn't seem to communicate at all. No sense in upsetting Olive unless I was sure this ghost was willing and able to tell her tale.

I didn't think she would be from the brief impression I'd gotten the few times she'd appeared.

I finished my notes then looked up at the other woman. "I think that's it for now, Olive. I'll call if I have any other questions. I'll also touch base in a few days to let you know how things are going—sooner if I get some information I think you need to know."

Olive stood. "You might want to come to Uncle Ford's viewing on Wednesday and possibly the funeral on Saturday. I know it's a long shot, but if this has something to do with David and my family…."

"I planned on coming by for the viewing anyway, to pay my respects."

Especially after I'd met DeLanie. I didn't know the rest of Olive's family, but viewings tended to be for those a bit removed to pay their respects—people who didn't feel they knew the deceased well enough to come to the actual funeral. And if Uncle Ford was that close to David, maybe someone else in Olive's family knew—someone close enough to have known Mary Allen and her possible connection to David.

I walked Olive to the door and went back into the dining room. Judge Beck looked up from his work, a resigned expression on his face.

"You heard?" I asked.

"I heard," he drawled. "Please promise me if this leads to some dealer in a dark alley, you'll put it in the detective's lap and step away. Please?"

I held up my hand. "I promise not to take on any drug dealers or street gangs." I sat down, but my mind wasn't on these skip traces, it was on that woman in the grave and all the different wild theories I could think of on how she'd gotten there. Leaving the judge to his work, I headed back to the parlor, to the tick-tock of my mantel clock, to my cat snoozing at the end of the sofa, to my knitting. Here I could think. Here I could just let my mind wander and hopefully come up with an idea of what I should do next.

I'd just started my knitting when my phone rang. Picking it up, I was surprised to hear DeLanie's voice. The woman sounded distraught as she identified herself, and her next words told me the reason why.

"I just read that the police identified the body they found in David's grave. It's Mary Allen. Can I hire you to investigate her death for me? I know the police are involved, but your card says you're a detective, and I need to know what happened. That poor girl. That poor, poor girl."

"You knew Mary Allen? She was a friend of David's?" I asked. My gut instinct had been right—the two *were* somehow connected.

"She was more than a friend. She was David's fiancée."

That, I hadn't expected.

CHAPTER 13

*D*eLanie handed me a cup of hot ginseng tea as I sat perched on a floral sofa, the guest book from David's funeral by my side and David's brindle bulldog, Beau, at my feet. DeLanie lived in a modest two-bedroom split-level on the other side of town—a house she proudly informed me that she'd bought thirty years ago when David was an infant and had just this year completely paid off. I envied her that.

"I'd only met Mary at the funeral," she told me. "Didn't even know her last name, but when I saw the picture online with the article saying that's who was in David's grave, I recognized her right away."

I reached down to scratch Beau behind the ears. "You met Mary Allen at the *funeral*? But you said they were engaged."

DeLanie sat down beside me, her own cup of tea in one hand and a photo album in the other. "You have to understand, David was always private when it came to his friends and social life. It wasn't just when he'd been using—he was always been that way. But when he came back from the last rehab this past Christmas, he was different. He was…fragile, vulnerable, more open. He told me then that he'd met a girl, and although it was early, he was sure she was the one. He asked me if he could use my mother's ring, and I told him yes. Went and got it for him so he'd have it handy at the right moment." Her mouth twisted and she opened the photo album. "He asked me if he could get the band inside engraved with their initials—M for her and D for him."

"But he never introduced you to her?"

She shook her head. "I thought maybe they'd broken up or something and didn't want to hurt him by bringing it up. Although he still seemed happy, he was never quite as glowing as he was over Christmas. He was stressed, you know? It's hard coming back from rehab. You want to do the right thing, but there's your old friends, and you've got to deal with all the mess you left behind the last time you were using. The slightest little stress and you start thinking about what a refuge those drugs were."

"She came up to you at the funeral? Introduced herself to you?" I winced, thinking how hard that must have been. The man you loved, that you were going to marry, was dead, and you were meeting his mother at his funeral.

"Yes. She said her name was Mary, and that she and David had been close, that she'd loved him and had wanted to marry him. She was wearing the ring. That's how I knew she was telling the truth, and that David must have proposed to her." DeLanie's eyes filled with tears. "He hadn't told me, and it was all my fault."

"What was?" I was confused, wondering why she would have thought a woman claiming to be David's fiancée might have been lying, and why his hiding the engagement was her fault. He'd gotten the ring from her. Maybe he'd only given it to her recently and had planned on bringing his fiancée over and introducing them over dinner or something more formal?

But then he'd overdosed and died.

"I didn't know her name or anything, but a few weeks before David died, Ford came by to see me. David was working at his company, and he said he was concerned about this girl he was dating, that someone had told him she was a druggie and bad news. He'd done some digging and told me the girl had a record, that he was worried she might make David start using again. Said he was going to talk to David about it." DeLanie sniffed and wiped her eyes. "Maybe that's why David didn't tell me they were engaged. Maybe he thought I wouldn't approve of her."

"Uncle Ford seems to have been really close to your son," I mentioned, giving Beau another quick pat on the head and sitting back on the couch.

DeLanie nodded. "David didn't have a father growing up, and Ford loves kids. He's got two of his own, although they're older. Olive will tell you, Ford was the one who would set up volleyball nets in the back yard, build tree houses, make homemade ice cream with the kids. He and David were close. He'd paid for David's rehab, sending him to a place I could never afford on my own. He got him a good job in his own company. He looked out for David. Ford took his death hard. The man was sick, really sick. He got diagnosed right after David's funeral and went downhill fast. I always believed in my heart that with David dying, he just didn't have the will to fight the cancer."

I thought of Madison and Henry and how I'd feel if something happened to one of them. It would be hard to go on about my life, knowing theirs had been cut tragically short, even more so if I were battling a terminal illness. Plus, Ford must have blamed himself. He'd done all he could for David, and still couldn't keep him safe from drugs.

I looked down at the photo album, at the adorable boy with his curly black mop of hair and dancing dark eyes in a round golden-brown face. His obituary picture had shown him to be a very handsome man, and as a child he'd been beautiful.

It was impossible to look at these pictures and connect this child, so very alive, with that body in the cemetery plot.

"Here's one of my mother wearing the ring." DeLanie paged back and pointed to a picture of an elderly African American woman, her hand in front of her mouth as she laughed. On her finger was a pretty ring with a modest sized diamond and a filigree setting on a plain white-gold band.

"It's pretty," I told her.

"It is, and David was so excited when I let him have it. About Mary, though." DeLanie sniffed and straightened her shoulders. "I know it sounds uncharitable of me, but she didn't seem well at the funeral."

"Not well? She was…" I frowned. "She was high?"

"I don't know. Maybe, or maybe it was just grief. I was probably really sensitive to it after losing my only child to a drug overdose. But you know…" she looked down, running her fingers over a picture of David jumping into a pool, "if they were engaged, then maybe they both relapsed. Ford could have been right about her being bad for David. But there at the funeral, with her wearing his ring, I didn't have the heart to confront her or kick her out."

"I'm so sorry," I told her, knowing how it felt to lose a loved one, although it must have been especially terrible to lose a child. No one should outlive their children.

"I can't really blame her, you know. Those days after David died, I seriously considered losing myself in drugs or drink as well. I didn't blame her, but I think maybe Ford did. She was at the reception after the graveside service, but when she left, I noticed Ford followed her out to the parking lot." She shook her head. "I'm sure he gave her an earful, poor girl. I hope the three of them are making amends up in heaven, because I hate thinking of people going to their graves without forgiveness in their hearts."

I frowned. "About what time was that?"

"Two? Three? The funeral was at eleven, so an hour for the funeral, the procession to the cemetery and the service there, then the reception at the church following…yes, it was probably closer to three because we were winding up when she left."

Speaking of winding up, it was close to eleven at night, and all of us had to work in the morning.

"It's really late," I told her as I gave Beau another pat, gathered up my purse and the funeral guest book, and got to my feet. "I should be going, but I'll let you know if I find anything. In the meantime, please take care of yourself, okay? This has got to have dredged up a lot of sorrow."

She nodded, her and Beau both walking me to the door. "I wasn't going to ask for the ring back. It was the last thing David gave her. But if she was wearing it…" DeLanie grimaced. "This sounds horrible, but it was my mother's ring. If she was wearing it, do you think I could have it back?"

"I'll let the police know about the connection, and tell them she was wearing a family engagement ring. Her family will probably be coming down for her effects and to make arrangements, but I'm sure they'll return the ring once they know."

"I'd like to meet them," DeLanie blurted out. "Can you give them my contact information? David loved their girl enough to put a ring on her finger, so I'd like to meet her parents."

"I'll make sure they get your information, and I'm positive they'd want to meet you as well."

I headed home, lost in thought and dealing with a lot of dredged up sorrow as well. And I wasn't all that confident I'd be able to help Olive and DeLanie solve this mystery. Bob

Baughman claimed they weren't aware of Mary's body in the grave, and Melanie claimed the cemetery had nothing to do with it either. If it had been someone from the outside as Bob had alluded to, that disposed of the body there and partially buried it, we might never discover who. It wasn't like the cemetery had security cameras or anything.

I'd do what I could, and hopefully the police would be able to solve this at their end. I'd do what I could, but the best I was hoping for right now was getting DeLanie back her ring and hopefully putting her in touch with another set of grieving parents to discuss a love that never made it to the altar.

CHAPTER 14

*M*orning came way too soon, and I'll admit I skipped my morning yoga. On the way into work, I called the sheriff's department and left a message for Miles, figuring it would be quicker to get information from him than from regular police channels. He showed up promptly at eight, right before the coffee had finished brewing, and the crestfallen expression on his face as he realized there was no basket of baked goods next to the coffee maker made me laugh.

"Rain check?" I asked.

"Kay, you're a muffin tease," he lamented. "I broke three speed limits getting over here."

Muffin tease? Oh my, that sounded positively lurid, which I'm sure was not what the deputy had intended. But his comment reminded me—I had some matchmaking to do here.

"You're a cop. You break speed limits all the time. Besides, I never said on the message there were baked goods involved as a reward for your information. Not everything in life is quid-pro-quo, buddy."

He sighed, looking at the empty spot beside the coffee maker. "Well, it should be. So what information are you trying to not-bribe out of me with muffins and scones?"

"Before we get to that, I've got a question for you." I waited until he'd filled a cup with coffee and I had his full attention. "Do you know Violet Smith?"

He thought for a moment. "Is she the one that just started working over at the courthouse a few months ago? The Smith girl that hasn't murdered, or stolen, or gotten into a fistfight with her neighbors, or got drunk and ran her car into the middle of the Durden's living room."

"Oh, like Rose is the only one who's ever driven into the middle of the Durden's living room. That's why they finally put that huge boulder out front. It's a wicked curve in the road, and people go too fast."

Miles scowled. "People who've lived here all their lives should know better than to go fast around that curve. Rose was drunk as a skunk. I don't even think she *was* speeding when she missed that curve, that's how drunk she was."

How had we gotten onto the topic of Violet's less-than-law-abiding siblings? "Okay, but Violet hasn't broken any laws. She's got a degree in accounting. She's passed her CPA exam. She has a job at the tax assessor's office and has a very promising future in forensic accounting." I shot Miles a significant glance. "She's young, pretty, and I think you should invite her out to dinner."

Was that rushing things? I don't know. I'd never done this matchmaking thing before—well, besides J.T. and Daisy, and J.T. was already completely on board with that pairing.

Miles stared at me for a moment, his coffee forgotten. "I don't even know what she looks like. I just remember seeing the name in the paper when she got the courthouse job. How does she know me? Did I meet her somewhere?"

I had no stinking idea. "I'm sure you've met her in passing. She's blonde. Pretty. She's got that wholesome girl-next-door look."

"All the Smith girls look like that," he told me. "And they're all bad news."

I was beginning to think this was a terrible idea. *And* I was beginning to think Miles was a horrible snob. "Okay. Forget about it. I just thought you guys would suit, but clearly I was wrong." On to the other reason I'd asked Miles to stop by. "So, who's the detective on the Mary Allen case?" I grimaced. "Please don't tell me it's that jerk Desmond Keeler."

The deputy took a sip of his coffee, trying to hide his smile. "He's a Milford City detective, Kay. Mary Allen's body was found in Locust Point, so it falls under the Sheriff's Department. And Keeler isn't a jerk, he just has a problem with civilians sticking their noses into investigations and doing things like, oh, getting themselves locked in a dumpster by a murderer, or insisting that he charge a dying old man based on circumstantial evidence."

"You don't have a problem with those things," I reminded him.

"I do have a problem with those things, but I'm easily bribed with muffins and scones."

I remembered Detective Keeler's fondness for baked goods, although he didn't seem to have quite the enthusiasm for them that Miles had. Perhaps I hadn't yet found his Achilles' heel. Maybe he was a pie sort of man.

But that didn't matter because he wasn't in charge of this investigation, and hopefully I wouldn't be finding myself working with him in the near future anyway.

"Chuck Norris," Miles suddenly announced.

"Huh?" I blinked, wondering if impressive martial arts skills or movies had a bearing on the Mary Allen case.

"He's the detective assigned to the case."

Miles sounded a little bitter at that, making me realize he was still harboring a resentment that he'd gotten stuck with charity-golf-tournament duty while the other deputies got called in for a murder.

"Chuck Norris," I repeated, thinking perhaps I'd heard him wrong.

"Yeah. Chuck Norris."

"You seriously have someone at the Sheriff's Department named Chuck Norris?"

"Yes, we do." He grinned, setting down his coffee mug and heading for the door. "Actually, I've got no idea what his real first name is. It starts with a *C*, judging from the nameplate on his desk. Detective Norris. Everyone calls him Chuck because it's funny."

Miles headed out, and I wasn't far behind him, driving over to meet the man in charge of the Mary Allen murder investigation. I didn't realize quite how funny the nickname was until I was face-to-face with Detective Norris. The guy really *was* a dead ringer for a young Chuck Norris. Detective Keeler might have that steely glare down pat, but I found this guy far more intimidating, probably because the whole time I was with him I kept imagining him tossing bad guys around the room.

"You're Miles's muffin lady," he said, eyeing my hands which were not holding any muffins. "You might want to start putting Stevia in those things or making low-fat bran or something because Pickford looks like he's gonna break the scale at his next physical."

That was totally unfair. Miles was starting to get a bit of an early-onset, childless man, dad-bod but that wasn't my fault. And he was hardly going to be breaking scales. Although carrying a few extra pounds to this lean-mean-fighting-machine was probably a worse crime than murder.

"I'm Kay Carrera with Pierson Investigation and

Recovery Services," I announced, deciding to ignore both the muffin lady comment and the one about my enabling Miles's weight gain. "Deputy Pickford tells me you're in charge of the Mary Allen case?"

He shot me a narrow-eyed glare. "Keeler warned me about you. Stay out of my case."

We were clearly off to a good start. Why couldn't homicide detectives be more like Miles?

"Too late. The family of David Driver has hired me to find out who was responsible for desecrating their loved one's grave with the body of a murder victim. I have information. You have information. We could both solve our respective cases a lot quicker if we cooperated. And, not to bribe an officer of the law, but there might be some pastries in it for you sometime in the near future."

The glare never wavered, but I got the feeling he was far more interested in information having to do with his case than any apple spice muffins I might be bringing by in the future.

"Okay. You go first," he told me.

I hesitated, then realized I wasn't going to hold back even if he decided to be a jerk and not answer my questions. Ultimately, I wanted the murderer and his or her accomplices caught and justice delivered and withholding information wasn't the way to see that happen.

"Mary Allen was David Driver's fiancée."

There was a moment of silence. I felt rather smug that I'd managed to actually impress Chuck Norris.

"We knew there was a boyfriend and were actually considering him as a suspect, but I guess not if he predeceased her." He nodded as if he were conceding a solid blow from a sparring opponent. "We hadn't even gotten his name yet. These Narcotics Anonymous people take that anonymous thing pretty seriously it seems."

"You have to admit, this changes things," I told him, pushing my luck on the impressing-Chuck-Norris front. "David Driver's grave wasn't just a conveniently open spot to dump a body. They were connected. There's a reason the killer chose to put Mary Allen's body there instead of leaving her in the woods in a shallow grave."

"Or it was the perfect place to hide a body, and the killer was amused by the irony of it all." Detective Norris sat on the edge of his desk, still looking like he might at any minute get up and throw someone across the room. "We've been pursuing that there might be a connection though. They were both recovering addicts. Mr. Driver died of an overdose and although we don't have tox screens back yet, it's not a stretch to assume we'll find some trace of narcotics in Miss Allen's remains as well."

"Possibly," I admitted. "Ms. Driver did say she seemed a bit out of it at the funeral."

His eyes widened—just a fraction, but I noticed it. "Mary Allen was at the funeral?"

"Funeral graveside service and the reception at the church following. By Ms. Driver's estimation, she left around 3pm."

And now his eyes narrowed to slits. "How did Ms. Driver feel about this girlfriend of her son's, given that she probably contributed to his renewed drug usage and subsequent overdose?"

I rolled my eyes. "She felt sad and sorry for the girl. DeLanie Driver didn't kill Mary Allen. She was shocked and shaken to find out the woman was dead. She's hardly the sort of person who would desecrate her beloved son's grave by murdering his fiancée and throwing her body on top of his casket. And besides, why would she agree to exhume her son's body if she'd dumped a body on top of it?"

"Maybe she murdered the girl and thought it was a sick

sort of justice to bury her with the son she believed Mary killed. Maybe she murdered the girl and whoever found the body knew and thought it was poetic justice to put the body in the grave of the murderer's son."

Instead of calling the police. Right. I was beginning to wish Desmond Keeler had this case after all. He was a jerk, but at least he wasn't an idiot.

"Uh, no. DeLanie Driver isn't a murderer. Mary Allen left the reception at the church around three. DeLanie was still there, and I'm willing to bet she wasn't alone until long after dark. Mary Allen died sometime after three o'clock and was in that grave by the time the contractors arrived to fill it in—which was most likely between eight and nine at night. That's a pretty short window of time, and I'll bet my socks that DeLanie has a rock-solid alibi. And Ford as well."

Oops. Maybe I shouldn't have mentioned Ford. Although I *did* want to help the police catch this murderer.

"Ford?"

"DeLanie's cousin's husband. He was upset that David was dating Mary and was worried she was going to make him relapse. He'd talked to David about his concerns a few weeks before he died and evidently went into the parking lot after Mary Allen left to confront her."

Chuck clicked his pen and pulled a notepad toward him. "And where can I find this Ford?"

"At the funeral home. He's the one who died last week. The one they were excavating David Driver's remains for, so he could be buried in that plot. And it wasn't him. He'd been ill for a while before the funeral and shortly after was diagnosed with an aggressive cancer."

"Doesn't take a lot of strength to shoot someone," Norris commented.

"It does to dispose of a body," I shot back.

He shrugged. "Maybe his wife helped him."

"Sarah? She's the one who insisted David's remains be relocated so Ford could be interred in the grave plot. She'd hardly do that and uncover where she'd stashed a body, would she?"

Man, this guy really was an idiot.

"Maybe not." Detective Norris sighed and shook his head. "Guess I'm back to tracking down other junkies as suspects."

"That's all you have?" I scowled. "Maybe if you find out who partially filled in that grave before the contractors got there, you could catch the killer?"

"I already spoke to the contractors and the cemetery manager. And not only did I review the camera from the main gate, I've spoken to everyone who came and went between the time of the Driver funeral and when the gravedigger guys arrived." He stood and made a motion with his hand as if he were pushing me toward the door. "There's no smoking shovel pointing to any of the three dozen people who had access to that cemetery so far, so I'm pursuing other angles. If you'll excuse me, I need to get back to work."

This time it was me who narrowed my eyes and glared at him. The jerk. He wasn't an idiot after all. The detective had totally played me. I'd just given him all my information and got zip in return.

"One last thing," I said as the detective herded me toward the door. "Two actually. The ring Mary Allen was wearing is a family heirloom. As she's deceased, Ms. Driver would like to have it returned. And can you please ask her parents when they come down if they'd meet with Ms. Driver? David and Mary were engaged, and she'd like to at least make their acquaintance and express her condolences."

"The second one, yes. The first one, no."

I bristled, hesitating even though the detective was beginning to invade my personal space in an effort to get me through the door. "Why not? Because it's evidence? Personal effects to be returned to her family? Should Ms. Driver ask them directly for the ring?"

Detective Norris gave me that heavy-lidded, stern look the actor was so famous for. "No, because the victim wasn't wearing any rings. Well, beyond earrings, that is. Thank you for your help, Mrs. Carrera. Have a nice day."

Somehow, I was outside the station, on the sidewalk, staring through the glass doors at the detective's retreating form.

No ring. They'd left her with a wallet that included ID, credit cards, and cash, but had wrestled a ring off her finger —a ring that although an heirloom, it probably wasn't all that valuable. If a killer was going to rob her, why go halfway? Or not even halfway?

There was only one reason—that ring meant something to the murderer. In spite of my protests to the contrary just a few minutes ago, that fact made me shift my thinking completely around. The ring meant something to the murderer—and the only people I could think of that would value an old antique ring with a small, moderate-quality diamond would be the family it came from.

CHAPTER 15

*I*t couldn't have been DeLanie ~~that~~ *who* killed Mary Allen. It couldn't have been.

Or could it?

Maybe she was bullied into moving David and pretended her shock and surprise when Mary's body was found. She *did* have motive. Her son's relationship with Mary might have led to his taking up drugs again. But why bring my attention to the ring if she was the murderer? Why make a big deal of it and ask to have it returned if she'd yanked it off Mary's finger after killing her? It didn't make sense. No one would have thought twice about the ring or even known about it if she hadn't told me.

Ford? I had scoffed at the idea of Sarah helping him, but surely the man had other family and friends who could assist him in covering up a crime. There was one hitch in that theory, though. My experience with men was that most of them couldn't tell one piece of jewelry from another. Maybe Ford was different, but I doubted he'd seen that ring and known it was his wife's aunt's. And why would he care about a piece of jewelry that had belonged to his wife's aunt anyway? It seemed implausible, even if he'd been the sort of man who appreciated women's jewelry.

Who then? Aunt Sarah? I couldn't imagine she'd be distraught enough over David's death to kill his fiancée in some sort of revenge for luring him back to drugs and then go on to insist that David's remains be removed, uncovering her murder victim's remains. No, Sarah didn't seem a likely murderer either.

Olive's parents? They'd grown up with Sarah and DeLanie, but I had no idea their names or their relationship with their family beyond Olive saying her father really didn't want any of the grave plots.

Or…. David's father wasn't named on the birth certificate, and according to Olive, he'd vanished out of DeLanie's life before his son was born, but what if that wasn't the truth? Maybe he'd recently discovered that David was his and had been secretly meeting with his son, only to be so devastated by his death that he killed the girlfriend that led his boy back to drugs.

I felt a bit sick that all of my scenarios so far had the motive of Mary's killing as revenge for David's death. Honestly, I had no idea if she'd even been using again, in spite of Detective Norris's confidence in what the tox screen results would be. Perhaps she had started using again and her dealer offed her for not paying or some other drug-gang reason. Or maybe she was clean and I was maligning the poor woman's memory. Maybe there was someone else who wanted her dead and was angry enough to throw her into David's grave—like an unstable ex-boyfriend.

Suddenly my imagination was filled with ideas of an ex discovering Mary's engagement and assuming once David overdosed that she'd return to him. He'd confronted her after the funeral, but instead of falling into his open arms, Mary had said "no". And he'd killed her. And thrown her body into the grave of the man she'd preferred.

Oh, that was a much better scenario than a mysterious father or one of Olive's relatives. And an ex-boyfriend who knew about the engagement might rip the ring off Mary's finger, not to keep it for sentimental reasons, but to take from her the one thing that linked her to David.

Yeah, there were some bumps in that theory, like why take the ring and put her in David's grave? Unless the final revenge was for him to hock it at a pawnshop for a dollar, like the mythical jilted wife and the husband's Porsche.

Starting my car, I pulled out of the station parking lot feeling a bit better. Detective Norris may have gotten the upper hand in our conversation, but I had some ideas and a clear course of action right now. I was going to break the sad news to DeLanie about the ring and ask her the details of which recovery meetings David liked to frequent. And while I was at it, I was going to ask her some uncomfortably personal questions about David's father.

* * *

DeLanie cried when I told her about the ring. Her tears were so genuine that any doubt I'd had about her innocence was laid to rest.

"It was my mother's ring," she told me with a sheepish and somewhat watery smile. "It wasn't worth much, but my father had scraped and saved to buy her that ring and she cherished it. So did I. I know it's silly, but the thought that some murderer took it off the hand of the woman my son loved…."

"I know," I told her. "I feel terrible about that."

"If they find the murderer, do you think they'll find the ring?" she asked.

I winced. "I hate to crush your hopes, but there's a good chance the killer threw it away or sold it at a pawn shop. I'm so sorry. I just don't want you to think it's going to turn up only to be upset when it doesn't."

She nodded. "Then I hope the murderer sold it at a pawn shop and someone loved it and bought it and is enjoying it right now. The important thing isn't the ring; it's finding out who killed Mary and put her in David's grave. That's what matters the most."

I took a breath and decided to delay the most difficult question for last. "I'm going to try and see if I can find any of David and Mary's friends, people who knew them best. Do you know which recovery meetings he went to? And was there anyone there he spoke about? Someone that might be willing to talk to me?"

DeLanie thought for a moment. "He told me once he liked the meetings over at the Lutheran church on Tuesday and Thursday nights the best. There was a leader there, Rudy, that David said he connected with. He always went at seven in the evening. Gave him time after work to change and get a bite to eat before heading over."

"Rudy. Was there anyone else he mentioned? Did he have a sponsor?"

"I'm sure he did, but he never mentioned his name. Maybe this Rudy was his sponsor? He lived here with me after he got back from this last rehab, but he'd gotten his own place over on Wilford Avenue a month before he died. A grown man needs his privacy, you know? Not living with his mother." DeLanie smiled. "Although I loved having him here. I always felt less anxious when he was under my roof. I felt like I could keep an eye on him, see him before he left for work and when he came home, and see him on the weekends. I could intervene if I thought he was having a hard time staying clean. I wanted to keep him safe, just like I did when he was a little boy. But of course he wasn't a little boy anymore, and I needed to have faith, not just in God but in David too—faith that he could take care of himself without me clucking over him all the time."

"Were there any other meetings he liked to go to?" I asked. "You said he went five times a week."

She nodded. "The ones on Tuesday and Thursday with Rudy were his can't-miss meetings. The others he just went when he had the need. I know some days he'd drive out at lunch to one. Weekends he'd find one in Milford or wherever he happened to be at the time. I think if Rudy would have had seven meetings a week, David would have gone to them all. But the other ones outside of Tuesday and Thursday were just to keep him toeing the line."

I took a breath, steading myself for the hard question I could no longer avoid asking. "Who was David's father?"

A look of grief flitted across DeLanie's face. "It don't matter. I raised him with help from some caring family. That's what's important."

"Did his father know he had a son? That you'd been pregnant with his child?"

"He knew about David. It doesn't matter who he is. It's not important. The only important thing was that David had people that loved him in his life—lots of people."

"But what if after all these years he suddenly decided to come into David's life? What if you didn't know that he'd been secretly contacting David? If I just knew his name—"

"He died, Kay. He died and there's no need to dredge all this up, to name names or anything like that. David's father had nothing to do with Mary Allen's death."

Well, there went that theory, although it had been a weak theory amongst other weak theories.

But with that theory gone, I was a bit concerned that I was rapidly approaching a dead end.

* * *

I HEADED BACK to the office and my skip trace work, but throughout it all, I couldn't help but think of David Driver and Mary Allen. At three o'clock I put on another pot of coffee and pushed my files aside, retrieving the guest book from David's funeral as well as the photo album DeLanie had loaned me from my car.

I was looking for either a woman who might have wanted Mary's ring, or an ex-boyfriend with a grudge, because I seriously doubted an angry drug dealer would have killed Mary and yanked the ring off her finger, only to leave cash and a bank card in her wallet. Opening the guest book, I pulled out a notepad and began to jot down any names that might be a possible murderer.

I should have just jotted down the names that obviously weren't the murderer because that would have been easier. I didn't know ninety percent of the people who'd signed this book. Some of the signatures were illegible. I was sure a good number of them were people who'd attended the viewing and were co-workers or possibly distant family friends paying their respects. This was *not* the way I was going to narrow down a suspect pool.

I eyed the skip trace files, but picked up the photo album instead. It was heartrending to go through all the pictures. DeLanie as a young woman. Her with a group of other children, who from the resemblance I assumed were Sarah and Olive's father. Her and her parents. Her and an adorable baby David, her face full of joy and love as she held her infant close. The rest were all David with his cousins. I recognized Olive in a few pictures.

Throughout it all, I felt as if I knew David. I felt as if I'd seen him grow from infant to young man. I'd seen him in his graduation cap, seen him fishing and playing in the sand, seen him in a tux going to prom, heading off in a dilapidated Honda to college, seen him hugging his mother, his eyes haunted and sad.

I paged back to the early days, hoping to catch a glimpse of something that might stir my intuition and point me to Mary's killer, but there was nothing. Paging back further, I found myself entranced by the pictures of DeLanie before she'd had David. The woman was roughly my age, and I felt a stab of nostalgia seeing her clothing and hairstyle, so close to what I would have worn at that time. And her parents...they reminded me a lot of my parents that I missed so much. I wish my mom were still here to talk to about Eli's loss, about things that were going on in my life. I wished that my father were here to gather me in his arms and tell me that everything in the world was going to turn out right.

I ran a finger over the page, pausing at a close-up of DeLanie's mother with her hand up against her cheek. The woman's wedding band and engagement ring were clear as could be in this picture, and I admired the pretty old-fashioned cluster of small diamonds and the white-gold band. Back before people shelled out insane amounts of money for Hope-diamond sized solitaires, many an engagement ring was this sort of cluster, or even of semi-precious stones. DeLanie's mother's ring was beautiful and well-crafted even if it might not have had the highest quality stones.

And it felt oddly familiar.

I thought about the engagement ring—this very engagement ring that had been on Mary's finger. I'd been envisioning the killer taking it off her finger, but perhaps she'd done that herself before her murder? Maybe after the funeral, she'd gone home and with a sense of bitterness and grief, had taken off the ring?

But then I looked at the picture of DeLanie's mother in the album, the ring glittering on her finger. Then I looked down at my own left hand where I still wore my wedding band as well as the diamond solitaire Eli had given me.

No, Mary wouldn't have taken it off. Not immediately after her fiancé's funeral, anyway.

CHAPTER 16

I parked outside the Lutheran church, walked up to the door, then hesitated. After dinner, I'd told the judge where I was going. He noted down the exact location and time of the meeting, making me promise that I'd text him promptly at eight to let him know I was still alive and what time to expect me home, making it clear that if I were more than two minutes late, he was calling the police. I had every intention of talking to Rudy and maybe a few of the other attendees about David and Mary, but now that I was actually here, I was having second thoughts.

Watching everyone enter, I felt as if I were intruding on something private. These people were here to share their struggles with addiction in a safe space. A non-addict showing up to ask questions seemed really disrespectful.

A man appeared at the doorway. He looked to be in his forties with a bald freckled pate and a bushy reddish-blonde beard. His blue eyes were kind, as was his smile. "Session starts soon. Come on inside."

"I'll just wait here," I told him, thinking it might be better to pop in when I thought their meeting was ending, to ask questions later. People socialized after these things, didn't they? Drank coffee and chatted before heading back home?

"You can't do it alone, you know. No matter how hard you try, you can't do it alone. No one in there is going to judge you, and you don't even have to share if you don't want. Just come in. Take this one step, and the next one will be easier."

Oh, no. I completely felt like a fraud now. "I just...there's someone I was hoping to talk to," I told him. "I'm not an addict."

"Admitting is supposed to be the first step, but you don't need to admit anything to be welcome here. Come inside. Just this once, then you can decide what to do next."

More guilt. "I'm really not an addict. I'm a friend of David Driver's cousin and his mother. I had some questions about David and Mary. His mother said this was his favorite meeting—this and the Thursday night one. He spoke highly of Rudy."

The man took a step back, eyeing me uncertainly. "You're the police?"

"No, a friend of the family. I do work for Pierson Investigation and Recovery Services, though." I could see him wavering. "DeLanie, David's mother, was so upset to find out Mary was dead, and the circumstances...she was there when they uncovered Mary's remains. She'd met Mary at the funeral, knew that Mary and her son were engaged. This is personal to her. It will help put her mind at ease, help her grieve, if she knows what happened."

"No one here knows what happened," he insisted.

"But you all *did* know David and Mary, and maybe something that helps us find out what happened—friends they hung out with, problems they were having with certain people, anything that might shed a light on what happened to

Mary and why someone went to the effort to bury her in the same grave as David."

He hesitated. "Let me ask the others. I'll be right back."

I waited and it wasn't long until his head popped back out the door. "We voted, and you can come in to join us. Please treat everything you hear inside as confidential, unless someone gives you permission to share their story. And I appreciate your being honest with me." He opened the door wider, ushering me in and extending his hand. "I'm Rudy, by the way."

I shook his hand. "Kay Carrera."

I followed him down a hall and into a room that held six people of varying ages and ethnicity, all hovering around a coffee machine and a bowl of those mini chocolate bars.

"Help yourself," Rudy told me. "Fresh coffee, and Lottie brought chocolates. We usually just have those mints, so get the good candy before it's all gone."

The others chuckled at his comments, making way for me at the coffee machine and eyeing me with a sort of wary curiosity. I filled a cup, adding powdered creamer and a packet of sugar, then took two of the chocolates before heading over to a circle of metal folding chairs.

The others came and sat, a woman I assumed to be Lottie bringing the bowl of candy with her to pass around during the meeting. I unwrapped a candy and popped it in my mouth, taking a sip of my coffee and trying to look supportive but unobtrusive. How did that Melanie at the cemetery manage this sort of demeanor day in and day out? It was hard to appear the right mix of caring but somewhat detached, a sympathetic onlooker who could remain in the background but be available if needed.

I sat off to the side and listened as the meeting progressed, moved by the struggles these people faced each day to keep their fragile hold on recovery. When they were done, Rudy announced that anyone who wanted to speak to me about David or Mary should feel free to do so.

A few attendees expressed how much they missed David and Mary, how upset they were at David's death, and how shocked they were about the recent news of Mary's murder. Every one of them shook their heads sadly and said they'd thought David was going to make it, that he'd been under a lot of stress, but happy and in love, and of all the recovering addicts they knew, they never expected to hear that he'd started using again. Equally, they were convinced that Mary had also seemed not at risk for relapse, although when David had died and she'd stopped coming to meetings, they'd assumed the worst. And now they felt guilty that the whole time they'd been thinking she was using, she'd been killed and buried in David's grave.

None of them knew anyone who would want to harm Mary. She was sweet, kind, and caring and didn't seem to have an enemy in the world. They all liked David as well, but several admitted pragmatically that someone who'd just put aside his habit might have more than one unsavory character in his recent past.

It made me wonder if instead of Mary contributing to David's death, he'd contributed to hers. Maybe instead of looking at Mary and the couple's current group of friends, I should be looking a bit back—back before David went into rehab this last time.

As everyone filtered out of the room, I helped Rudy put up the chairs and clean up the coffee cups. He turned out the lights, then we walked together to the parking lot behind the church.

"Mary's been coming for a long time," he finally told me as he walked to a blue Honda parked under a tree. "She had some trouble right out of high school. Got arrested. Didn't serve much time, but it definitely was a wake-up call. Seven years that woman's been straight from what I could see. She was solid. Regular meeting attendance. Absolutely dedicated to helping others recover. That's how she met David." A smile ghosted across his face. "At one of my meetings, actually. That's where they met. Made me feel like I was some sort of Cupid."

His words surprised me. I'd been expecting Mary to be a woman who struggled with her addiction, one who might have been on shaky ground and the bad influence that DeLanie and Ford had thought she might be.

Rudy leaned against his passenger door and continued. "They met this past winter. David came to a meeting out of the blue—first time I ever met him. He said he'd used that morning, but was leaving for rehab the next day and needed a connection, needed to know people were rooting for him while he was gone. He was scared, down, feeling like this trip was going to be a waste of money. I've seen people like that before. Sometimes they can pull themselves out of the hole, and sometimes they can't. Looking at David that night, I wasn't giving him good odds, but we were all there for him."

Rudy took a breath and stuck his hands in his pockets, looking up at the tree. "Mary talked to him after the meeting. Evidently, she left with him and they stayed up all night. She was with him every minute until he was on his way to rehab. And when he got back, she was there, too. She pulled him through that, gave him a rope to hold onto when he felt like he was falling. That first meeting after he got back, I could see the change in him. And I knew seeing the two together that they were in love."

I smiled, thinking what a wonderful love story this was. If only it hadn't ended so tragically.

"A few months later, she was wearing his ring. I know they had some tough times. There was some reason they were keeping their engagement quiet, and whatever that reason was, it was stressful to both of them. I thought maybe it was a racial thing or something—that one of their parents wouldn't have approved. Or maybe their family would have had a problem with it because both of them were recovering addicts. The reason wasn't something they shared, even in meetings."

"Did David ever talk about his father? Or any of his family?"

Rudy thought for a moment. "I know he was very proud of his mom for raising him. He had cousins he liked a lot. Some older guy, an uncle maybe, who'd kinda taken David under his wing when he was young. I remember David saying he paid for the rehab and that he was worried he was wasting this man's money, that he'd just disappoint him."

"How about Mary? Any family she mentioned?"

He shook his head. "Her parents were out of state. They moved about five years ago, and she'd stayed because she had a good job and felt secure here."

"Any particular people you know who were good friends of theirs?"

He chuckled. "The regulars all know each other, but most of them don't socialize outside of meetings unless they're helping one another through a rough spot. I was Mary's sponsor, and I can pass along your information to David's sponsor and ask if he'd like to contact you. Other than that, I can't say anyone at the meetings was more than just a fellow recovering addict on the same journey."

"Was there anyone they mentioned having a problem with?" I prodded. "I know people come to these meetings to talk about stressful situations that make them feel the urge to use again. Did Mary or David mention any of those? Problems on the job? With neighbors? Friends they'd needed to sever ties with?"

"Mary had some issues with her job, but I don't think it

was with any co-workers. I seem to recall it being more of mandatory overtime and busy-season thing. She was the shipping supervisor at Formidable Printing." He frowned. "She worked there for seven years. I wonder what they thought when she just didn't show up one day. Probably the same thing we did. Her fiancé dies, and she loses herself in the needle."

I winced. Did everyone just assume she'd started using? Did everyone simply write off her disappearance as a woman who'd turned back to drugs? Her parents had filled out that missing person's report, but no one else seemed to bother and *that* was a tragedy, not just the fact that her promising life was cut short.

"What about David? He worked for his family's company, but maybe there was someone there he wasn't getting along with? Someone who didn't like a family member getting a job he thought he should have gotten?"

"No. I do know Mary had an ex-boyfriend—someone she'd broken up with a month or two before she met David. I remember her talking about that. And now that I think about it, I remember her mentioning a few weeks before David died that there was an ex who was being a problem."

Bingo. "Do you recall anything about him? Name? Where he lived? Or worked? How did Mary say he took their breakup?"

"I really don't know. I know there was a boyfriend late last fall, and she mentioned a breakup—which I think she initiated. Then nothing else until this past spring when she said in passing that there was a problem with an ex." He shook his head. "I'm sorry. Sometimes people get very specific in their stories, but Mary and David didn't—probably because they had each other to confide in."

I fished a few cards out of my purse and handed them to him. "Please call me if you can think of anything. And can you pass one of my cards along to David's sponsor? And anyone else who you think might be able to help?"

He nodded, then turned to open his car door. "I will. I can't believe someone would have killed Mary. And this seems a bit personal, doesn't it? Being put in David's grave? It's not like some random mugger or rapist would do that. I hope they catch whoever did it because she was a nice person and didn't deserve this. Not that anyone deserves to get murdered, you know."

"I know." I thanked him again and headed toward my car, texting Judge Beck for the second time that evening that I was alive and safe, and this time was on my way home. As I drove, I thought about what Rudy had said. An ex-boyfriend.

I'd reached the end of the road here as far as checking family, friends, and those who had access to David's grave, but as I pulled in my driveway, I realized I'd made an incredibly stupid mistake. I'd gotten my investigator's license and jumped into this case like an old-fashioned gumshoe. That wasn't a bad thing, but I'd completely ignored the one thing I was really good at—and the one thing that might just help me find a solid lead to Mary's killer.

The internet.

CHAPTER 17

I moistened a paper towel and wiped the coffee from around the lip of my mug.

"Something wrong?" Judge Beck asked. He was fully dressed and ready for work in spite of the sleep still hovering around the corners of his eyes. From the noise coming from upstairs, Madison and Henry were still getting their clothes on.

"No, nothing's wrong," I lied. The dishwasher decision had been pushed into the background behind the far more pressing investigation, but I really needed to stop procrastinating and figure out what I was going to do because hand-washing dishes for two weeks wasn't remotely an ideal solution.

And if I was finding old coffee on supposedly clean coffee cups, I was very concerned what was still left on the plates and silverware.

The judge eyed his own mug. "I need to have a word with the kids about their dishwashing skills."

No, I needed to replace the darned dishwasher.

"It's okay," I told him. "I'll call the repair place today and tell them I'm replacing it instead. Maybe we can get a new one in by the weekend."

If I went with rusty-and-dented, or obnoxiously red, then we would definitely have it by the weekend. I mentally thought of my savings account, trying to decide which was the better option.

"Don't make a rash decision because my children seem to be unable to effectively wash dishes," he protested. "I'll talk to them. This is ridiculous. I grew up washing dishes by hand. Our parents washed dishes by hand. Centuries of humans have washed dishes by hand. It's not rocket science. They just need to be more thorough, to check when they're drying and putting them away."

"They have enough to do with homework and their sports after school. It's been almost three weeks. I'll just buy a new one."

The judge stared intently down into his coffee. "I meant what I said earlier, Kay. Let me just put it on my credit card, and you can pay me later."

"No." I tried to make that word firm, but not too firm, because although I'd turned the furnace on this morning and everything appeared to be working fine, I couldn't guarantee that I wouldn't need to take Judge Beck up on his offer at a later time for some other major, emergency home repair. "No, I went out and looked at dishwashers during lunch on Monday. I figured it was going to come down to this, and I've got a couple I'm interested in. I just need to decide which. I'll do it today. Promise."

Judge Beck took the kids off to school, and I headed into the office only to find I had two urgent skip traces that needed a priority rush job. Credicorp was paying extra for these, so I set the Driver case aside and got to work. They were both difficult cases, and I ended up working through my lunch, not even having time to make a decision and a purchase on the dishwasher, let alone to do my internet research on Mary Allen.

Finally done with the rush skip traces, I looked at the clock and barely had time to download a state case search as well as credit reports before racing out the door. Dinner was a rushed affair. While the kids were doing the dishes, I looked over the case searches, noting that neither Mary nor David had taken out any protection orders or filed a no-trespass charge against anyone. A quick glance at their credit histories didn't reveal anything shocking, but I'd have to take a more thorough look tomorrow morning. Right now, I had a viewing to attend.

"I'm going with you."

I looked up at Judge Beck in surprise. "To the viewing?"

He nodded. "Madison and Henry are finishing the dishes, then working on their homework. We'll be back before they go to bed."

"I know, but are you sure? It's a viewing for Olive's uncle. You hardly know Olive."

"She's been in our house several times visiting you and at both our happy hours and barbeque parties. She's your friend. I feel I should go as a show of respect."

Our house. Our happy hours and barbeque parties. Our.

"Okay," I told him, feeling a bit off kilter by his comments and the implications.

Judge Beck drove, pulling into a rather full funeral home parking lot and around back. We were both still wearing our work clothes—the judge in his suit and me in a pair of khaki pants and a silky tank with a navy jacket. Heading in, we signed the guest book and made our way through the crowd.

DeLanie was toward the front, over to the left talking to a group of young men. I saw Olive by a well-dressed couple not much older than I was. She waved us over and introduced us to her parents— Shirley and Oliver.

"Yes," Olive laughed. "I'm a junior. Dad didn't think he'd get a son, so instead of Oliver, I'm Olive."

"But you have a brother, don't you?" I asked.

"Branson." Oliver chuckled. "Seven years after Olive was born. He was a surprise, our miracle baby. I wanted to go ahead and name him Oliver, but Shirley insisted on naming him after her father."

"I wasn't having two children named Olive and Oliver as well as a husband named Oliver." His wife laughed. "You got your junior. My daddy deserved to have a grandbaby named after him."

"I should be glad I wasn't named Branson," Olive commented. "Although being asked where Popeye was my entire childhood wasn't exactly a picnic."

Olive escorted us around, introducing us to various family members. When we reached the front of the room, I saw a woman standing beside the casket. The resemblance between her and Olive's father was pronounced, making me realize this must be Aunt Sarah.

She was wearing a black sheath dress that had a row of decorative key-hole cutouts around the hem. Her gloves had the same trim at the wrists. Like many women in the room, she wore a hat—a round pill-box style with a wisp of lace at the edge. Her salt-and-pepper hair still retained quite a bit of its original black and was straightened into a chin-length bob.

As we approached, I noticed her carefully applied makeup did nothing to hide the grief in her red-rimmed eyes and trembling mouth.

"I'm so sorry for your loss," I told her after Olive introduced us.

She nodded, reaching out to grip my fingers with the hand that wasn't holding a balled-up tissue. "Olive told me you recently lost your husband as well?"

I nodded. "Eli. He passed in March."

"Just before David did." The words were soft and accompanied by a perplexing mix of sadness and guilt, along with a certain hardness in her expression. "We barely had time to deal with his loss before Ford was diagnosed. Six months later and he was gone as well. It was all so fast."

"It must be hard to suffer two losses in one year," I agreed.

"Do you have children, Mrs. Carrera?" Sarah asked, suddenly fixing me with an intense gaze.

"No. Eli and I were never blessed."

"Ford and I had two boys. He loved his children. He took his responsibilities as a parent very seriously, but it was more than just duty to him, you know. He loved his children, each one of them."

I nodded, not sure if I was to glean any meaning from that statement beyond her reassuring herself that her husband had been a good father. Although it was a bit odd that she hadn't added the usual "good husband" comments. Every relationship had their bumps, though, and I could tell from her obvious grief that she'd loved Ford.

"Will...will things continue as planned for Saturday's funeral?" I asked, not sure if the police had cleared the grave as a crime scene and moved David's remains yet or not.

"We're not sure yet." She uttered a soft, bitter laugh. "It would serve me right if the answer was 'no.' Some hurts never heal, you know. But the fires of old pain shouldn't be stoked back up again. Angry as I was over that grave plot, I should have let the boy lie in rest."

"But then no one would have ever known what happened to that woman. Her parents deserved some closure, even if her murderer is never caught."

Sarah sighed. "I fear more than one secret has been unearthed with that woman's body. And it's my own damned fault."

She turned to greet another guest, leaving me a bit confused. Judge Beck had held back in conversation with Oliver and Shirley. Olive had moved away after introducing me to her aunt and was over speaking with what looked to be a couple of work colleagues. Feeling a bit awkward just standing around, I walked over to the casket and paid my respects to a man I'd never known.

Olive's uncle looked peaceful in his repose, even though cancer had clearly taken the girth from a man who had once carried quite a few extra pounds. My gaze quickly moved on to the huge sprays of flowers decorating the casket and the pictures of Ford in his younger days.

The pictures beside the casket were fairly recent, but off to the left was a huge collage of photos that included some of a little boy fishing, riding in a wagon, standing next to other children. I followed the photographic story of Ford's life as a happy child and mischievous teen, only to halt at one showing a handsome man in his late twenties.

I stared, everything clicking into place. The resemblance was uncanny, and there was only one reason for there to be so besides sheer coincidence. Ford was related by marriage, not blood, but this picture told a different story.

A quick scan of the room allowed me to locate DeLanie. I made my way to her, thinking about Sarah's comments, about DeLanie's refusal to name David's father, about Ford's closeness to a child that had been an out-of-wedlock son to his wife's cousin.

"Can we speak a moment in private?" I whispered to DeLanie. She looked up at me, and from her expression, I realized she knew what I needed to discuss with her. Waving me into a side room, she carefully closed the door and turned to face me.

"Yes. David was Ford's son. And yes, Sarah knew."

"How…" Duh. I knew how. I was just so shocked that the

man I'd seen in the pictures would have cheated on his wife with her own cousin.

"It's not what you think," DeLanie told me. "About eight years into their marriage, Sarah and Ford were having trouble. They'd split up. They'd been apart for nearly a year and it looked as if divorce was likely. Ford and I...well, it just happened. We all grew up together, and looking back, I think he was searching for some comfort, and I was lonely after breaking up with a long-term boyfriend. We weren't together very long before he and Sarah decided to try to make their marriage work. I don't blame him. He always loved her, and they had the two boys together."

"But you were pregnant."

She grimaced. "That was a surprise. I didn't expect Ford to leave Sarah or anything, but I wanted to have that baby and keep him. I was willing to lie and say it was my ex-boyfriend's or some other man's. Few in the family knew about Ford and me, and I'm sure they would have accepted I'd gotten pregnant from a one-night stand or something. But Ford refused. He said he wasn't going to lie about his own child, and that he'd step up to the plate and love the baby just like he loved his other two sons."

"That was the rift between you and your cousin Sarah?" I asked.

"We didn't get along as kids, and weren't all that close even after we grew up. But yes, she was not only going to have to see me at family events and know that I'd had a brief physical relationship with her husband, as well as having David a constant reminder of that, knowing that Ford would shower the same love and affection on David as he did his and Sarah's two boys... it was unbearable."

"But the grave." I shook my head in disbelief. "Ford is part of your family by marriage, but David was by blood. You shouldn't have had to move him so Ford could have the cemetery plot."

"I got tired of fighting." DeLanie's shoulders slumped. "It's been a battleground between the two of us since she found out. With David and Ford both gone, I'd hoped to finally patch things up between us. I won't deny that it hurt, though. It's as though she wanted David erased completely from our family. And I'm not sure moving his remains is going to change how she feels."

I thought of the woman I'd just spoken to, how she did seem to harbor both guilt and the feeling that what had happened had been some sort of karma for her not letting go of past hurts. "Only time will tell," I finally told DeLanie.

"Probably." She sighed. "And I know how this looks. It makes Ford seem a top suspect in Mary's murder. He was upset over losing a son. He didn't want David to date a recovering addict. I know he thought that perhaps Mary was responsible for David's using again."

"Even a sick man can fire a gun," I told her. "And he may have had help disposing of her body."

DeLanie shook her head. "If Ford was angry enough to kill her, then he would have just left her wherever he'd shot her. He *never* would have put her body in with David. If he blamed her for his son's death, then putting her body in that grave would have been a desecration. It was someone else. Ford didn't do it."

If Ford was guilty, then the murderer was beyond earthly justice. But if Ford *had* killed Mary, then perhaps whoever helped him with the body could still be charged. And perhaps whoever helped him with the body wasn't all that attached to David. It seemed to fit—Ford kills Mary out of anger and grief over his son's death. Sarah finds out and doesn't want her husband to spend his remaining time in jail, so she disposes of the body in the one place no one would look for it.

Except Sarah didn't seem physically capable of hauling a body into her car, to the cemetery, across twenty feet or so to the open grave plot, then shoveling dirt on top of it. It just didn't fit with the woman out there beside the casket. And if she'd disposed of Mary's body in David's grave, she hardly would have insisted it be dug up and her crime exposed.

I was back to wondering who wanted Mary dead, and who either felt the grave was a convenient dump spot, or disliked David enough to think his grave was a fitting spot for a body disposal.

It brought me around to the ex-boyfriend again. And me with no clear way of figuring out who he was.

CHAPTER 18

I was in the middle of hacking into Mary Allen's Facebook account when Chuck Norris walked into my office.

This clearly wasn't a social call, and judging from our last meeting, I knew he wasn't popping in to update me on the case in the spirit of mutual cooperation. His presence in my office this morning meant one thing—he'd hit the same dead ends I had and was hoping to dig for information.

He eyed my screen, then pulled a rolling office chair up next to me and took a seat. "Find anything?"

I kept scrolling through Mary's friend's list. The key to seeing all of someone's social media posts was through connections. I just had to find that right friend of Mary's, the one with a gazillion friends and followers who automatically approved any and all friend requests, then sneak in through the backdoor, so to speak. Most people left a lot of information open to the public. Even more people changed their default security settings to share a lost dog flyer, then forgot to change them back, posting merrily away for months or years without even realizing their pictures of last night's dinner and updates on their foot surgery were there for the world to see.

Mary had been more careful. Outside of a few tagged pictures, very little of her posts were visible to me. I was hoping to change that, but Detective Norris didn't need to know that so far, I was hitting a big fat zero.

"So far, I've found out that Mary went to the lake a year ago last summer with some girlfriends, that she likes puppies and thin-crust pizza. You?"

He shifted in his chair. "Not much."

I turned to him. "I'm not going to tell you squat unless you cough up something more than 'not much.' You do know that, right?"

A sheepish grin spread across his face. "You learn fast."

I turned back to my computer, refusing to be charmed into spilling it all. "Tell me something I don't know or head on out that door because I've got work to do."

"You know, withholding information on a murder investigation isn't a good way to ingratiate yourself with the local police force."

I shot him a sideways glance. "It's hard for me to know what's pertinent when you don't share information. For all I know, Mary liking puppies was exactly the clue you were looking for."

The chair squawked as he leaned back. "Sadly, no. We're looking at someone who knew both David and Mary—knew them well enough to pick David's grave as a disposal site. That's too odd to be a coincidence."

"So family, friends, a jealous ex, someone from their mutual past who held a grudge," I added.

He nodded. "Although their mutual past was less than a year. Any of David's family who might have been a suspect wouldn't be pushing or agreeing to have that grave dug up."

"And Mary's family?"

"Alibis for the date and time of death and no motivation whatsoever. She's an only child. Her parents didn't know she was engaged, didn't even know about David, although they said she'd told them a few months before she went missing that there was some issue with an ex. She'd call them every month or so. When she hadn't contacted them as usual, and they couldn't locate her, they filed a missing person's report. Although they told me they feared the worst, they were adamant that Mary hadn't used since the time of her arrest at eighteen, then she'd stayed clean. No drugs. No alcohol. Regular church and NA meeting attendance. She cut out all her friends who were users and didn't even socialize much with those in her recovery group outside of meetings. Her parents were surprised when I told them Mary had met David at a meeting and that he'd been in recovery as well. They said that she'd broken up with someone last fall and told them she was swearing off dating for a while, wanting to focus on volunteer work supporting other recovering addicts instead."

It sounded like she'd done just that, only to fall in love with one of those she was helping. Again, I thought how horrible it was that what should have been a sweet love story had turned tragic.

"I'm looking for the ex-boyfriend as well." I pointed to the screen. "Maybe he was waiting in the wings, and after David died he thought there would be a reconciliation, only to become enraged and murder Mary when that didn't happen."

"Six months is a long time to wait in the wings," Detective Norris commented. "And she wasn't strangled, or bludgeoned, or stabbed. She was shot, which brings a premeditated component to this that you don't get with enraged, jilted ex-lover."

"So psycho, enraged ex-lover who brought a gun because if Mary said 'no,' he wasn't going to let anyone else have her,"

I speculated, because I really didn't have any other suspects on my list.

The detective shrugged. "I'll be straight with you here—do you know who David's father is? His mother isn't saying. There's nothing on the birth certificate. I'm wondering if he was back on the scene, connecting with his thirty-year-old son, and blamed Mary for the overdose."

Oh, I felt so smug to know the answer to this one. "His father is to be buried in that very grave this Saturday. Ford Branch."

Detective Norris blinked. "That's keeping it in the family."

"David's funeral was right before Ford's diagnosis of an aggressive form of cancer. He was very ill at the time. There's no way he could have murdered Mary and disposed of her body in his condition, and even if he had, I don't think he would have put the body of a woman he thought contributed to his son's death in his son's grave."

"Shot her, then felt guilty and buried them together?"

"I'm still liking the ex-boyfriend for this," I told him.

He stood. "Well, I'm still liking the father. His wife clearly didn't help him dispose of the body only to insist it be dug up six months later, but I'm sure the guy had other friends and family that would help him out. He had two other sons, right? I'm sure one of them would help keep his father out of jail and keep his mouth shut, and maybe he put Mary in David's grave without the father's knowledge."

It was a good theory—but mine was just as good. "So, you'll let me know what you find out?"

He eyed my computer screen again then dug a card out of his pocket and put it on my desk. "Only if you let me know what you find out there. I don't know anything about searching for stuff on those social media accounts. I'd be real curious to know what you turn up."

"Likewise." I pretended to be intent on the friends list as

the detective let himself out of the office. I would tell him what I found, whether he reciprocated or not, because I wanted the police to catch the murderer. I wasn't going to go running to him with a bunch of vague information and red herrings though. I wanted to prove my value to the local sheriff's department, and to do that I had to show them I knew what I was doing.

Mary's affection for puppies and pizza didn't seem to be a good lead, but I was curious about the lake trip. If she had close enough friends to go away for a long weekend with them, then they were close enough to share information with. I'd jotted down the people tagged in the pictures to speak to later, as well as the dates of the information I could access. If I could just develop a timeline, question a few of her friends, I could maybe find this ex-boyfriend of hers, the one she'd been worried about, the one whose anger had made her keep her engagement under wraps.

Reaching the end of the line, I sent a few friend requests to a few likely prospects, then looked up the profiles of the tagged women in the lake trip. Not wanting to fall into the black hole of non-friend messages, I noted their birthdates and the city where they lived, then headed to the state case search database.

I found that one had a wage garnishment. From there, I kept digging until I found a number that hopefully was still current and a place of business. Leaving messages on both, I set it all aside and called it an early day. It was Halloween. I had pumpkins to light, candy to set out, and Kentucky short ribs to make with Madison.

I got home by four, let Taco out for some free time, and did a quick bit of Halloween decorating with some old stuff I'd found in a tub in the attic. As I stabbed rubber hands into the dirt and hung plastic spiders from the porch ceiling, I remembered the first few years after Eli and I had bought this house.

I'd made decent money at the paper, and although he was raking it in as a surgeon, he still had some frighteningly large student loan debt to pay off. We both had car payments, although they were modest. This house had been our biggest splurge, our gamble that our finances would only improve and we'd be able to do all the repairs and enhancements that we'd dreamed of when the realtor had first shown us through the house. And of course, then we were still hoping to fill all these bedrooms with children.

The children never came, but we'd paid off Eli's student loans with some frugal budgeting, and as his income increased, we'd begun to make this house our dream home. But even those first years when money was tight, we'd celebrated Halloween with these very decorations I was putting out now, making sure we had plenty of candy for the kids who that came by.

Eli always overbought on candy. And he'd never gone for the cheap stuff, either. For weeks afterward, we'd had dishes of mini chocolate bars all over our house. I'd done my fair share to put a dent in the extra candy, but it was Eli who really loved the chocolate. After a few weeks he'd step on the scale, express his horror at the weight gain, then haul the three pounds of candy still left over into the hospital for the staff to eat. He'd usually come home that night laughing that it had all been eaten within three hours. No one likes chocolate like doctors, nurses, and hospital staff, he'd joked.

Judge Beck pulled in with the kids at quarter to five. They both raced inside—Henry to throw on a makeshift costume for what might be his last year of going door-to-door for candy, Madison to get started on her short ribs. The girl had been cooking for a while now, so I gave her some space, deciding that this was a simple enough recipe that she didn't need me hovering over her. After I finished putting up the decorations, I put the mini chocolates into a bowl and headed into the kitchen to check on my budding chef.

Madison was spooning the barbeque sauce over the short ribs, ready to put them in the oven. "Thirty minutes, put the salad in a bowl, and we'll be ready," she announced.

"Then you go sit on the front porch and hand out candy while I clean up some of these dishes," I told her. "I'll pull everything out of the oven when it's ready and make the salad. You go have some fun, and if you want to throw on a sheet and go trick-or-treating with Henry, go ahead."

She leaned over and surprised me with a quick kiss on my cheek, then ran as the doorbell rang. I got to work on the pots and pans, popping up front every now and then to catch a glimpse of the early trick-or-treaters.

I'd just pulled the short ribs out of the oven when my phone buzzed. I hit the speaker button and started putting the salad into a bowl.

"Kay Carrera." I'd expected one of those automated calls, a recording offering me a refinance of my non-existent student loans, or alerting me of a great deal on replacement windows. I didn't expect it to be Mary Allen's lake-trip friend returning my call.

"I'm Stacy Washington. You called me about Mary?" The woman barely took a breath before launching into a speech. "I can't believe…when I read in the paper that they'd found her body, that she'd been murdered…. I hadn't heard from her in months, but after David died, I just assumed she left to go live with her parents for a while. Now I feel like a terrible friend. She was dead and in that grave, and I didn't do more than send her a few texts? I never even bothered to find out if she was okay or anything. Oh, God, I can't believe she's dead."

"You went on a lake trip with her last fall, right?"

"Pfft. Yeah. Me, Mary, Leslie, and Eileen. Mary had just broken up with that slime bag Richard. Richard the Dick Hodges. We were celebrating. Best damned decision she ever made, well, except for getting clean, that is. We made more margaritas than a tequila bar on Cinco de Mayo. Swam. Grilled. Got one mother of a sunburn. Mary swore off men. Said she was going to become a nun and help other addicts. I'm sure that was the tequila talking, but she didn't take that loser back, and that's all that mattered."

"What did you think about David?"

She hesitated. "He was a nice guy. He treated Mary right, and I could tell she really loved him. When he proposed to her, gave her that ring, I think it was the happiest day of her life. But…"

I had girlfriends. I completely understood. "He hadn't been clean for very long."

"He hadn't been clean at all when Mary met him. And less than a month back from rehab and he's proposing? I don't wanna say he was the wrong guy or anything, but I wished she'd taken things slower, made sure he was solid in his recovery before jumping in with both feet, you know?"

"Were you worried Mary would start using again? That he'd falter and take her down with him?"

"Oh Lord, no. Mary was solid. Although after David died, I did wonder if she'd start up again. His death hit her hard. He was the only man for her, as far as she believed."

"How did Richard feel about the breakup?"

She snorted. "He got mad. Then he cried and begged her to come back. Then he got mad again. It went on for a few weeks, but he finally gave up or found another girlfriend."

"Do you think he was the sort of man who might have approached Mary after David's funeral and try to get back together with her? Someone who might be angry enough at her refusal to kill her?"

"Richard? Hardly. He was all bluster. The moment Mary stood up for herself, he folded into a blubbering begging mess of need. He's a dick, but he's not a killer. And for all his begging and crying, he's got too much pride to try to get Mary back after she'd moved on."

"But she told the people at her recovery group that she and David were keeping the engagement under wraps because of her ex. That doesn't sound like Richard was over her. That sounds like a crazy stalker ex who might resort to murder if he couldn't get his way."

She laughed. "That wasn't Mary's crazy ex, it was David's."

My mouth dropped open. "David's?"

"Yeah, I didn't get all the details. I'm not sure Mary even knew all the details. David had some ex-girlfriend that refused to let it go. I got the idea she'd been hounding him for a long time. Like years, long time."

Why hadn't DeLanie mentioned that? "Do you know when they'd dated? If it had been a recent breakup?"

Stacy made a frustrated noise. "From what Mary told me, the two of them had been off and on again for, like, the last decade. So no wonder the woman thought David was going to come back to her again. He always seemed to. It was another reason I didn't think he was the best match for Mary. But she loved him, and she was absolutely positive he was done with the ex once and for all. She said David just needed a few months for the ex to cool off and all would be okay. Richard hadn't been an issue, so Mary was convinced David's ex would be the same."

But then he died. And then she was murdered. Although I wasn't completely willing to give up on Mary's ex as a murderer, David's ex was now at the top of my list.

"Do you know what her name was? This former girl-friend of David's?"

"Mary never said. Maybe one of his family or friends know? I'm sorry. I wish I could be of more help."

"Can I call you if I have any more questions?" I asked her.

"Yes, please do."

Stacy hung up. I grabbed the platter of short ribs in one hand and the bowl of salad in the other and headed into the dining room. Tonight was all about family and celebrating the spooky holiday, but tomorrow morning first thing, I was going to need to ask DeLanie a few more questions about her son and possible past girlfriends.

CHAPTER 19

"*D*avid dated a lot," DeLanie told me. "He wasn't a player or anything, but he kept things casual enough that he didn't introduce any of them to me."

"But he didn't introduce Mary to you either, and he was planning on marrying her, so it's not a stretch to think he would have an on-again, off-again relationship with someone and not tell you?"

"I figured a lot of his girlfriends were users and he didn't want me to know about them. As far as I know, his girlfriends only lasted for a few months. He was probably single more than he was with someone."

"Did he ever mention one that he felt was a problem? One that wouldn't take a breakup as a permanent thing?"

DeLanie thought for a moment then slowly shook her head. "No. I know there was a girl in high school that he was friends with. She went to the same college as he did. I got the impression from him that she had a bit of a crush on him. I think they may have gone out here and there, but I don't think it was anything serious. That's the only thing I can think of that would have been remotely considered on-again, off-again."

It was such a setback that David hadn't been on any social media. It made it hard to even find pictures of him through tagging. But as DeLanie talked, an idea came to me.

"Did David have a cell phone? Do you have it and know his password?"

She nodded. "Yes, I have a box of his things in my room over here. I never could get rid of them, but didn't even want to put them away. It just seemed like he was near as long as I kept his things around." She went over to a box and went through it, pulling out a phone and handing it to me. "I don't know where the charger is. David always used the same password for everything—1215. It was my birthday." Her voice broke on the last sentence.

Returning to the office, I found a charger in J.T.'s desk drawer that worked, plugged in David's phone, and sat down to find Richard Hodges. I quickly discovered that Richard had no criminal record, had a rather spotty credit history, and a job at Dickerson Construction that he'd held for the last five years. He had a Ford F-150 with alarmingly high payments. He had a little rancher he'd bought over in Milford three years ago.

And he had a wife.

I frowned at the screen. Richard Hodges had gotten married in April to a Leesa Vasquez. Well, Richard certainly hadn't wasted any time. He'd gone from angry and begging Mary to not leave him to married to another woman in six months. Although to be fair, Mary had found love just as quickly after her and Richard's relationship had ended.

Richard's social media was fairly bare-bones, but his profile pic was a wedding one. His new wife had wedding and honeymoon pictures splashed all over multiple sites. I still might have thought there was something that might have tied him to Mary's murder—blackmail or revenge, or old feelings of love and anger dredged up by a death and a marriage. The only thing that made me cross Richard's name off my list was the timing. His wedding was three days before David's funeral, and according to the pictures all over his wife's accounts, he and Leesa were in Aruba during Mary's murder. Nothing says alibi like eighteen hundred miles of distance.

Stacy was right. It wasn't Richard. And unlike Detective Norris, I refused to believe that a terminally ill Ford had shot his son's fiancée and elicited help in disposing of her body. No, I was leaning toward the ex-girlfriend.

Who no one seemed to know about.

I eyed the stack of skip traces. Then I turned back to my computer and found the Locust Point High School yearbook from twelve years ago. There was David, handsome as ever and looking even more like a young Ford in these pictures. I downloaded a list of the graduating class, then, wanting to start by casting a broader net, I downloaded the list of the following year's graduates as well. DeLanie said this girl had gone to high school and college with David, but she might have been a year younger.

David had gone to State. I didn't have time to go through all the hoops of getting the college to send me their enrollee records for the four years David was there, so I fired up a handy little bit of software that J.T. had purchased when he began to take on skip trace clients. We paid a fee each time we used it, but for those hard-to-find people, this software was invaluable. I set the parameters, then let the software crawl through social media and search engine data, doing in a few hours what would have taken me weeks to do manually.

Then I turned to David's cell phone, hoping his mother had been right about his password. It turned out I didn't even need the password. David's phone fired right up, showing me a picture of him and Mary, cheek to cheek. Her hand was on his chest, a diamond engagement ring front and center on her left-hand ring finger.

They looked so happy, and for a moment, tears stung my eyes. They didn't deserve this. They should have been married, had kids, grown old together. It wasn't just Mary's murder that upset me either, it was David's life being cut short by his addiction. All the photo albums, discussions with his family, what I'd pieced together off the internet.... David had not been a troubled child, destined for this sort of end. He'd been happy, active. He'd played sports in school, gotten good grades. His mother had worked two jobs, but between her and Ford, he'd grown up right. He'd done well in college, graduated with a business degree and an entry-level job in marketing with a local tech firm. There he'd gotten regular pay increases, and a promotion. I was certain he'd attended the occasional party, had joined his friends for happy hours, possibly drank too much at a weekend barbeque, but nothing in his youth or young adult life foreshadowed a drug addiction or his overdose death.

Had he started abusing prescription drugs after needing them for something so common as back pain or a root canal? Had the emergency room given him opioids after that car accident six years ago, and he found himself unable to give them up? Had that addiction quickly slid into the cheaper heroin? An addiction even rehab and the love of a woman in recovery couldn't break? It seemed such a heartbreakingly common story. I'd grown up thinking addiction was a crisis of the poor, but the last few decades had seen those claws grabbing hold of middle-class America. No one's child, sister, uncle, or spouse was immune, it seemed.

"Oh, David," I murmured as I scrolled through the texts

on his phone. "If only you hadn't died. If only someone had gotten to you in time, been there to help you."

But he had died. And Mary had been murdered the afternoon of his funeral. And all I could do to help them now was find Mary's killer and see justice served.

The texts were an interesting mix of work-related communications, a few regarding recovery group meeting recommendations from a man who I assumed was David's sponsor. There were some from Ford. One from his mother back in January asking him to pick up milk on his way home. Most were from Mary, and I felt a bit guilty as I delved into their personal conversations.

They started in December, right before David had gone to rehab this last time. At first, they were warm and encouraging, but obviously texts between strangers—Mary reassuring David that he could do this, that she and the group would be there for him when he got home, to catch him if he felt himself falling. There was a gap in the messages where I assumed David had been in rehab and unable to use his phone. When they started up again, the change in tone was rapid and marked. The two quickly fell in love, David touching in his honesty about his struggles and Mary his rock. They discussed more than a shared addiction, they talked about family, work, what food they liked to eat, an early morning snow, a squirrel at the bird feeder. Between the long message threads and pictures, I felt I actually knew these two people.

The words of affection and love grew more frequent. And with them was concern over someone they both called CW. She'd called David again—five times in one evening. She'd showed up at his house, at work. He'd thought she might have broken into his apartment a few times. Mary wanted to confront her, but David didn't want his fiancée to become a target. He told her to be careful, that he'd take care of it, that

CW had assumed they were getting back together once David got back from rehab, that he blamed himself, thinking he might have said things while he was under the influence that had led this CW to believe they had a future together.

Mary wasn't so charitable. She urged David to call the police, told him she didn't like this sneaking around. Never once did she chastise David for having possibly led this woman on. She did, however, express concern that the stress of dealing with this ex might jeopardize David's recovery. The texts ended on that note the day David had died. The final three messages were from Mary, asking how something had gone, then frantically urging him to call her. I felt ill looking at them, knowing what had happened, imagining Mary's grief.

Had Mary confronted this CW and accused her of driving David to use again? Had this ex been so unstable and fixated on David that maybe she killed the rival for his affection out of anger and grief? Reading these texts, I had more than a strong suspicion that this unknown woman was the murderer.

CW. I looked at my crawler software that was still chugging along, then went through the high school records, searching for a woman with the initials CW. There was nothing in David's graduating class, but in the one the year after, there had been a Cindy Weiss.

That had to have been her.

Firing up J.T.'s computer, I hunted for anything I could find on Cindy Weiss. She hadn't gone to the same college as David, but perhaps DeLanie had been wrong about that. She was cute, with dark hair and a bright smile, the sort of girl I could see David dating. Nothing about her online presence sent up any alarm bells, but people sometimes hid their true selves well.

But it quickly became clear that Cindy Weiss wasn't the

murderer. Right after college she'd gotten a job at an IT firm out in California and moved there. And there she'd remained, marrying, having two children, and joining the local Rotary Club. It couldn't be her.

I went back to the high school records, expanding out a few years, but unable to find another CW. Maybe DeLanie had been wrong about the high school? Perhaps this on-again, off-again girlfriend had gone to Milford High instead?

Feeling like I was searching for a needle in a haystack, I prepared myself to search through half a dozen county high schools when the computer dinged, announcing that my friend request had been accepted.

Picking the less onerous of the searches, I hopped over to my new friend, Eileen Mack's page and scrolled back to the time when Mary Allen was still among the living. Two cups of coffee later, I found what I'd been looking for, although it wasn't what I wanted to find.

Mary had commented on one of Eileen's pictures that she'd probably be announcing an engagement soon. Eileen had replied that Mary needed to announce hers first, if only they could get rid of Crazy Woman.

CW. Crazy Woman.

My heart sank, realizing that CW wasn't the ex's name; it was short for Crazy Woman. I picked up David's phone again, frustrated that they'd never named this woman, that I'd have no way to find her. There was no sense in digging through Milford High or other school records. I no longer had a name to search.

But maybe I didn't need a name. David had said in a text to Mary that CW had called him five times in one day. Scrolling back, I made note of that day and went over to the section of David's phone that held the records of incoming and outgoing calls.

Thankfully the man had bought a phone with a ton of

memory and never seemed to bother deleting anything, because the number was right there, clear as day. It was assigned to a contact in his phone listing, making me wonder if he'd deleted CW from his phone when the relationship was over, or if the ex had gotten a new phone. I jotted it down, started to type it into the computer to search, then decided to take the bull by the horns.

You can imagine my shock when a female voice answered the phone—a calm, sympathetically cheerful, detached voice.

"Windy Oaks Cemetery."

CHAPTER 20

"*U*m, hi." I stuttered, my mind whirring. "This is Kay Carrera. I'm just… I'm just checking to see if the Branch funeral tomorrow…if the interment is going to be as planned? I mean, did the police clear the crime scene, or is the family holding off on the interment?"

I thought of Melanie as I'd made arrangements for Eli's funeral, thought about how calm, sympathetic, and detached she'd seemed. A smiling automaton that said all the right things, but never seemed to actually *feel* for the client in front of her. At the time I'd thought it an admirable trait, her way of coping with a job that landed grief at her desk twenty-four/seven. Now her demeanor seemed a bit off.

And at David's gravesite she'd had that same unemotional, vaguely sympathetic expression. I frowned, trying to recall her expression when Mary's body had been discovered. No shock, certainly. No, that calm demeanor had never once cracked even after the body was found.

Maybe because she knew it was there all the time.

Oh, God, the ring. She'd had on a necklace, been fingering the chain— the only sign of emotional distress she'd shown.

The pendant hanging might not have been a pendant, it could have been a ring.

"Yes, the police have cleared the grave. We're preparing it this evening and I'm happy that it will be ready for the Branch funeral tomorrow." Her voice oozed with cool kindness and flat cheer. I shivered.

"Did...Was David Driver moved?" It was odd that Olive or DeLanie hadn't called me about that.

"We've just gotten the okay to move him. Mrs. Driver is coming down this afternoon to watch over the re-interment. It's all on a very short timeline, but we're so happy we could accommodate our clients in their time of need."

"Yes. We're so happy. You all are wonderful. Thank you," I babbled, hanging up the phone and staring at it for a moment.

Could I be mistaken? This just seemed so farfetched, that the manager at the cemetery was a murderer. She certainly had opportunity to dispose of the body right there where she worked. But did she even own a gun? And motive? I had no proof that she'd had any contact with David or Mary beyond her professional duties.

I checked the high school graduation and saw that Melanie had been the year behind David. But so had hundreds of other women. Maybe she'd had a good reason to call him that day. There were no voice mail messages for me to check. Maybe David had been getting a price on cemetery plots? Or maybe she was in one of his recovery groups?

I picked up the phone again and called DeLanie, confirming that she had indeed received word that David's remains would be moved this afternoon. Olive would be there, and I eagerly accepted her request that I also attend. Then I got down to the question spinning around in my brain.

"Melanie Swanson, the manager at the cemetery, did she

know David before his death? Were they in sports together, or friends, or did he have some reason to be in contact with her at the cemetery?"

DeLanie thought for a second. "Well, I'm sure he did know her. A couple of years ago when that mess started over the extra grave plot, he went down to the cemetery to see if they had anything documenting who it should have gone to in the family. Why?"

"She went to Locust Point High School the same time he did, and there were some calls from her office at the cemetery to David a little over a year ago."

"That could have been her following up on the grave plot issue. I mean, I'm sure David knew who she was. Locust Point High School isn't very big. I don't remember them being friends when he was in school, or them dating or anything, but maybe after. David met a lot of people through rehab and his meetings, too. I've got no idea if she was one of them, but I've been surprised by some of the people who were in recovery from drug or alcohol addiction and kept it all secret."

I told DeLanie I'd meet her at the cemetery, sat back to think through my "evidence." Of which there was pretty much none. I had no proof that Melanie had ever dated David or harbored any sort of secret, psychopathic crush on him. They'd gone to school together. She had a legitimate, non psycho reason for the phone calls last year. All I had was a series of what could be coincidences, and the fact that as the cemetery manager, she'd be perfectly positioned to dispose of a body in an open grave.

I made a call and dumped the entire thing in Detective Norris's lap. As I went over my research process, and my suspicions to his answering machine, I began to feel like a fool. I should stick to skip tracing and the occasional divorce case. This sort of thing was way beyond my abilities. It was slow methodical police work that would eventually, hopefully, uncover Mary's murderer, and as much as I wanted to be the one triumphantly revealing the solution to this crime, I wasn't Jessica Fletcher or Miss Marple. Or even Nancy Drew.

I got back to work on the few remaining skip traces, texting Judge Beck to let him know that I might be late getting home tonight. At three o'clock I wrapped everything up for the weekend and headed to the cemetery. Olive and DeLanie were already there, standing by David's gravesite. The police tape was gone, but the canopy was still there as were the chairs, the digger, and the apparatus to haul the liner and casket up to transport it to the new plot. Three men with shovels stood next Melanie over by the truck.

The ghosts were still there. It felt like their numbers had grown since last Saturday. They were like a disapproving mob, hovering all around the open grave. I hoped Olive was right and that they'd go back to wherever they normally were once David's remains were relocated, but having them here was unnerving.

"I hope you're not waiting on me," I told DeLanie.

"No, just some final instructions for the workmen," she replied. "There's not much more digging to do, then they'll bring up the entire liner and put it on that vault truck there. We'll follow it to the new gravesite that's prepared and ready, then watch them lower it in. That Melanie woman said it shouldn't take more than half an hour."

I put a hand on her shoulder. "Are you doing okay?"

She shrugged. "It's not easy watching people dig up your son, knowing his body is inside a casket in that big chunk of cement. I'll be glad when it's all over."

The excavator started up, the two men with shovels standing by as the man began to scoop out dirt with the careful precision of a surgeon. Melanie walked over to us after a quick glance down in the grave plot, her usual calm, unemotional expression in place.

I looked at the chain around her neck, at the hint of a circular pendant I could see just under the collar of her blouse. She shifted and a bit of silver flashed into view. It was a ring. I could tell it was a ring, but was it *the* ring? How could I get a better look at it without being too obvious?

The excavating part of the disinterment was quickly over and the workmen moved the digger to the side, pulling the vault truck up and lowering the claw-like apparatus into the plot. Two men jumped down with straps to secure everything in place, then hopped back up to give the go-ahead. Slowly the liner emerged from the grave—a large concrete rectangle pitted and covered in dirt. As it rose, the workmen at the graveside came forward to secure the straps and guide it onto the waiting truck.

The whole time I kept glancing over at Melanie, trying to see her necklace without seeming like some weirdo looking down another woman's shirt.

We followed the vault truck in a procession to the newer part of the cemetery, only fifty feet or so from where Eli was buried. There another plot had been prepared, a second canopy in place as well as chairs. This Melanie might be a murderer, but she was a very effective cemetery manager.

We stood a safe distance from the plot while the workmen carefully lowered the concrete liner into the opening, removing all the straps and bringing in the digger to close the grave. I glanced over at Melanie again, at her necklace. Could I comment on it and pull the pendant into view before she jerked away? What in the world could I possibly say to excuse such an action? *"Oh, I just love silver chains. Let me see your necklace?"* Yeah, because that was just the sort of thing someone would do after witnessing the relocation of someone's remains.

DeLanie took a deep breath and gave us a watery smile. "He's home. And I feel so much better now that it's done. Thank you both for coming. And thank you, Miss Swanson, for making this such a smooth process." She reached out to shake Melanie's hand, then changed her mind and hugged the woman instead.

There was an expression of sheer horror on Melanie's face, as if she expected DeLanie to plunge a knife into her chest. She patted the older woman awkwardly on the back then stepped away. That's when it happened. The silver chain caught on DeLanie's scarf, extending in a line between the two women. And dangling from the end of the chain was a ring.

The ring.

DeLanie looked down, raising a hand to disengage the chain. She froze, her gaze locked onto the ring. Melanie grabbed it in a fist, yanking it and nearly ripping DeLanie's scarf in the process, but before she could hide the ring back under the neckline of her shirt, DeLanie reached out and gripped the chain.

"That's my ring. That's my mother's ring. Where did you get that?"

I'd never heard that tone of voice from DeLanie before. Melanie paled and tried to pull away, but Olive and I stepped in on either side of her.

"What?" Olive asked. "What ring?"

"The engagement ring," DeLanie told her. "She's wearing the engagement ring around her neck on a chain. It was my mother's, and I gave it to David. He gave it to Mary, even had her initial engraved on it. I'd know it anywhere."

"It's mine," Melanie countered. "I bought it. I bought it at a pawn shop months ago because it was pretty and had my initial on it. It's mine."

"Then let's see it." Olive had a steely edge to her voice.

The workmen glanced over at us with some curiosity but didn't interfere. Finally, Melanie's fingers loosened, revealing the ring.

"It looks like the one in your family pictures," I told DeLanie. "And the one Mary was wearing on David's cell phone."

"I'd recognize it anywhere," she replied, picking it up and looking at the engraving inside. "DD and MD—David Driver and Mary Driver. That's how David had it engraved."

"It's mine," Melanie insisted once more. "I bought it at a pawn shop. I'm sure I have a receipt for it somewhere. Maybe. It was months ago. I might not have kept the receipt."

"Well, hopefully you bought it on your credit card or have a cancelled check," I told her as I pulled my phone out. "Because you're in possession of a murder victim's ring, and I'm calling the police."

* * *

A DEPUTY TOOK our statements while Melanie accompanied Detective Norris to the police station to give hers. We were all back at my house in time for Friday happy hour on the porch, which this week was our way of comforting DeLanie and celebrating David's new home at Windy Oaks Cemetery. Everyone clustered around with their wine while the three of us lifted our glasses in toast to David and began to talk about the ring.

"Maybe she did buy it at a pawn shop," DeLanie commented. "I mean, we did speculate that the murderer may not have kept it, that he might have tossed the ring or sold it. If so, I'm glad this way I'll at least be able to get it back."

"I think she's lying," Olive said. "She was always weird, even back in high school."

"You knew her back in high school?" I asked, astonished.

"She was a couple of years younger than me, but yes. I used to feel a bit sorry for her. The kids made fun of her because her family owned the cemetery and that they were living in the caretaker's house. Spooky Melanie, they'd call her. Or Lurch. She *was* kinda weird, though."

"But why would she have killed Mary?" DeLanie asked. "I don't remember her having any connection with David."

Olive shrugged. "Maybe she knew the murderer, gave him a convenient spot to dispose of a body, and at the last moment, snatched a pretty ring off Mary's finger."

"Or maybe she was obsessed with David and snapped when he got engaged," I countered. "Friends of Mary's say they were keeping the engagement under wraps because he had a psycho ex-girlfriend. Maybe Melanie was that psycho ex-girlfriend."

"Hopefully that detective will figure it out," DeLanie said. "I didn't find anything in David's effects that would make me think he was dating her, or anyone really. He didn't even have any pictures of Mary, just some of him and the dog, his fishing gear, and clothes."

"He had one of Mary as the wallpaper on his phone," I told her. "It seems like no one actually prints out pictures anymore, they're all either posted up on social media or on their cell phones."

"And David didn't do the social media thing," Olive commented. "I tried to do an announcement for our family reunion on Facebook a few years back, and I had to actually mail the man a paper invitation."

DeLanie chuckled. "Well, he sure seemed to print a lot of pictures of his dog. I must have found hundreds of them in his bedside table. Four years of pictures starting the day he adopted that dog from the shelter. He might have put a ring on Mary's finger, but I think that bulldog of his was the real love of his life."

"How *is* Beau doing?" Olive asked. "He must miss David terribly."

"He's doing better. He moped around for a few months after David died, but he seems to be happy with me. He's such a good boy. I actually like having him around."

I knew how she felt. I'd gotten Taco right after Eli had passed and having an animal really made the house feel less lonely. And in DeLanie's case, I'm sure the dog reminded her of her son.

Happy hour was winding down by the time Judge Beck got back. I told Olive and DeLanie that I'd see them at tomorrow's funeral, then went in to do some knitting while the judge and Madison fixed tacos for dinner.

Tacos. The dishwasher. Crap, I'd completely forgotten about it. Taking out my phone, I dialed the used appliance store, thrilled that they weren't closed yet.

"Hi, this is Kay Carrera," I told the woman. "I was in earlier this week, and I've made a decision. If I give you my credit card number, do you still think you can have my dishwasher installed Monday morning?"

CHAPTER 21

udge Beck had headed off for Henry's soccer game, making me promise once more that I wouldn't confront any drug dealers or murderers at Olive's uncle's funeral. I lingered over coffee and muffins, let Taco in from his morning outdoor time and fed him, then went upstairs to shower and put on an actual dress for one of the few times in my life.

Luckily, I had a nice subdued, long-sleeved, black knit dress that fit. I did my no-fuss hair, my equally no-fuss, minimal makeup, slid on a pair of modest-heeled pumps, and headed out.

I was glad for the modest-heeled pumps because I had to park halfway down the road from the funeral parlor and walk there. It seemed Ford Branch had been a well-loved man. I waited in line to get in the door, waited in line to sign the guest book, then entered a huge room that was practically standing room only full of people. I promptly got in the receiving line to see Sarah behind a man wearing a baggy suit that looked like he'd had to pull it out of mothballs for this occasion, and a short, fat, striped tie.

"Did you work with Ford?" the man asked me.

"No, I'm a friend of the family," I told him. "Did you work with him?"

He nodded. "We all loved Ford. He was an amazing boss. Fair. Kind. Smart. His son Len is a good guy, but I'm gonna miss having Ford around."

I guessed that Len took over the business when his father got ill. It reminded me that David had also worked for Ford when he'd come back from this last rehab.

"It's heartbreaking that they've lost two family members this year," I commented. "Did you know David Driver? Ford's...cousin? He'd started work this past January and died I think in March?"

The man nodded again. "I knew David. He was nice. A hard worker, too. Seemed to have everything together. Met his fiancée. She stopped by the job site looking for him a few times."

"Mary." I was surprised that she'd come by David's work.

"No, that wasn't her name." The man frowned. "Melanie. She was weird, in my opinion. Told us she was engaged to David and was asking about when he was working and what sites he was on. The next day I told David she'd been by and he seemed upset by it. Told me to let him know if she came back. She didn't, so I guess he talked to her about showing up at his work." The man shook his head. "Some women are strange like that. They're always thinking you're cheating or something and having to check up on you all the time. Better not to get mixed up with someone like that, you know?"

I caught my breath. It was the connection Detective Norris would need. Melanie could claim she'd gotten the ring from a pawn shop, but her showing up at David's work? Asking about him? She had to be the crazy ex that Mary's friends had been talking about.

"I'm Kay Carrera," I told the man, sticking out my hand.

"Steve Polk." He shook my hand while I committed his name to memory. As soon as the funeral was over, I needed to call the Sheriff's Office and have Detective Norris get in touch with Steve Polk over at Branch Building and Electric.

I gave my condolences to Sarah and was looking around for Olive or DeLanie when I saw a face I recognized—someone I hadn't expected to be at Ford Branch's funeral.

"Miles," I said once I'd made my way over to the deputy who was wearing a navy suit that looked like he might have last worn it to his high school prom. "I didn't realize you knew Ford."

"I…uh, yeah. Not well, but thought I'd come pay my respects, you know."

I eyed the deputy, thinking that he was a horrible liar. "You're here working, aren't you? Undercover, I assume?"

He let out a breath. "No, I'm here to attend a funeral."

"Well, tell Norris he needs to talk to Steve Polk at Branch Building and Electric—that's Ford's company. The man said that a woman named Melanie had shown up at one of the job sites before David Driver's death claiming to be David's fiancée and asking about which job sites he worked at and what hours he worked. See? They knew each other more than professionally. And Melanie has motive if she was claiming to be David's fiancée. Maybe she felt jilted and killed Mary out of jealousy, then snagged the ring she felt should have been hers."

Miles turned aside and whispered. "We're checking the pawn shop records she said she bought it from, but nothing was ever filed on that ring. Pawn shops have to file with the police for every single thing they buy or take as pawn collateral. It's the law, and there's nothing on the report that matches that ring."

"So you *are* here on business," I whispered back.

"Keeping an eye out in case something happens," he said,

scanning the room.

"Me too," I told him.

"Hey, I went by the courthouse the other day," he told me. "Stopped by the property tax office."

My eyebrows shot up. "And?"

"I think Violet Smith is pretty. And smart. And she doesn't seem at all like her sisters, except they all look alike, you know. But beyond that, she…. well, she's hot."

Score two for my matchmaking success. Well, if Violet liked him back, that is. "Did you ask her out?"

His grin was more than a bit sheepish. "No. Not yet. I was hoping you'd put in a good word for me first. I'm not exactly Don Juan when it comes to the ladies, you know."

I patted him on the shoulder. "Miles, you're adorable. And yes, I'll call Violet next week and put in a good word for you. Stop by the office around Thursday or Friday and I'll let you know what she says. I'll even bring muffins."

"Double chocolate?" He gave me a sideways glance.

"Apple spice," I told him. "Now do your job and catch a murderer."

"I'm trying."

I moved away to find Olive and DeLanie. The two women and Suzette were off to the side of the room, looking at the collage of Ford and in particular looking at the picture where I'd seen the resemblance between him and David.

"That Melanie woman did it," Olive whispered to me. "I've been thinking about it all night, and I'm sure she did it."

"I agree," Suzette whispered as well. "I think she's guilty of murder and of dumping that poor woman's body in David's grave."

"The police are checking the pawn shop and I found someone who said she was coming around David's work claiming to be his fiancée and asking about his hours," I whispered back. "I think Melanie did it, too."

185

Olive recoiled. "He may have dated her, but David wasn't a player. He wasn't the kind of man who would lead two women on with promises of marriage. He never would have proposed and given Mary that ring unless he'd completely broken things off with Melanie."

"If there ever *was* anything going on with Melanie," I told her. "It could have been all in that woman's head for all we know, some kind of crazy unrequited love."

A muscle twitched in Olive's jaw. "She's not here at the funeral, but she'll be at the interment. She's always at the interment. And while she's there, I'm going to sneak into her office and see if she's got pictures in there of David, or of Mary, or letters or something."

"Me too," Suzette added. "She was bold enough to wear that ring on a chain right in front of everyone. I'll bet she's got other things in her desk."

"Probably," I agreed. "And I'm sure the police will find them. They'll get proof she was lying about the pawn shop, then they'll talk to this co-worker of David's and have proof that she knew David, that she had motive, then they'll get a search warrant and find this other stuff."

Olive shook her head. "She'll probably have gotten rid of it by then."

"The woman that was wearing Mary's engagement ring around her neck?" I scoffed. "I don't think she *can* get rid of anything. You heard her at the cemetery. She kept insisting the ring was hers. I think in her head she really believes David was going to marry her. After he died, she probably snapped on Mary."

"Or Mary confronted her for stressing David and pushing him over the edge on his recovery, and Melanie shot her," Olive added. "Either way, I want to make sure she's not hiding evidence before our slow-as-molasses, Mayberry-like police force gets around to searching her office."

"Don't," I urged. "Her lawyer will counter and say you planted pictures there or something else. Just let Detective Norris do his job."

I can't believe I was saying this, the very person who stuck her nose into every murder investigation. In a way I did agree with Olive. The police might get their search warrants too late, after Melanie had hidden anything incriminating. I'd searched social media like a bloodhound and not found a smoking gun. A ring and stalking a guy at his workplace were a big leap to murder. It was all too flimsy, too circumstantial for the police to make a murder charge stick.

Smoking gun. Mary had been shot. If Melanie had killed her, that gun had to be somewhere.

"I'm doing it," Olive insisted.

"Me too," Suzette chimed in.

I wavered for half a second—truly only half a second. "Okay, but I'm coming with you two."

Olive gave me a quick smile. "Good. I was hoping you'd say that. Now come with us. They're about to start the funeral service."

I sat in between Olive and DeLanie, and as the minster described Ford's life, I felt tears sting my eyes. This was the first funeral I'd been to since Eli's and the reminder was hard to ignore.

I missed him. I missed Eli so much. There were days when I wasn't sure what to do with myself, how I'd possibly go on without a man who'd been my whole life. Then there were days when I felt like I was on the verge of something new and wonderful—not better than my life with Eli, but different and just as amazing.

But here, with the casket and the music, and the minister, and the scripture, I felt my loss like a sharp knife between my ribs.

After the service, I pulled my car into the procession line

with my lights on and drove slowly through town and into the gates of the cemetery. Once there, I veered off to the left, making my way around the outer roads and toward the newer section in the back where the offices were located. I parked my car next to Olive's and got out to stand next to her and Suzette.

"Are you sure about this?" I asked Olive. "You're missing your uncle's graveside service and we might not find anything."

"I'm sure," she said with a sharp nod. "Uncle Ford would have wanted justice done. He would have wanted David and his fiancée to rest in peace knowing their killer was paying for her crime."

I agreed. "Then let's go."

The three of us headed into the building and I turned right, leading Olive and Suzette to the office I knew was Melanie's. The door wasn't just unlocked; it was wide open. With a quick look around, Olive and Suzette headed for the desk while I checked the various knickknacks and other items on a shelf by the door.

The books were clean, in alphabetical order. They were the sort of gilt-lettered, leather-bound books that someone bought to display but not read. Just like the unexciting art on the walls. It reminded me of Melanie—cool, unemotional, efficient. It was hard to believe a woman like that could murder someone, but I'd seen her face when Olive hugged her. I'd seen her face when Detective Norris had confiscated the ring.

It was hers, she'd claimed. And she'd been a boiling pot of rage about the detective taking something she felt belonged to her. Then just as quickly as the emotion appeared on her face, it was gone, leaving the usual cool placid expression in its place.

"We found something," Olive hissed. "Here. Letters."

I came around the other side of the desk where Suzette had used a tissue to pull some letters from a drawer. The top two were from David, insisting that their brief relationship was over and that she stop calling him. The next one was from David informing her that if she showed up at his work again, he was going to the police. The next one was him begging her not to make trouble, to just leave him alone. Not to hurt Mary.

Hurt Mary? Had Melanie threatened to harm the woman? I eyed Olive who nodded grimly. This combined with the ring and David's co-worker's testimony might be enough.

There was more. The next stack was a bunch of letters that Melanie had evidently sent David and had somehow retrieved from him. They were letters of love that later on became letters threatening to kill Mary if he didn't return to Melanie. David was hers, and she wasn't about to give him up.

"Whoa," Olive softly voiced.

"He was *mine*."

The three of us jumped at the voice, looking up to see Melanie standing in the doorway.

"She stole him from me. He was mine, and that cow stole him." Melanie took a step into the room and I moved away from Olive and Suzette, thinking that two of us might need to tackle this woman while the other one got away.

Oh Lord, I hoped she didn't have that gun.

Melanie took another step forward. "When David died, that stupid cow he was dating saw me at the interment. She came after the reception at the church to see me. She blamed me, said if I hadn't been stalking him then he never would have turned to drugs again." Melanie's laugh had a rough, hysterical edge to it. "Me! He was fine until he met her. Yeah, he was using, but he had it under control. Then he met her and suddenly he's too good for me and doesn't want to see me anymore. She stole him from me. That ring should have been mine. I loved him for years, and *I* should have been the one wearing his ring. Me."

I stepped around the desk, holding my hands so she could see I wasn't carrying any weapons. "I know how you feel, Melanie. I lost my husband this year, remember? I know how much it hurts to lose someone you love."

A shadow formed just behind the woman—a ghostly form that I'd come to recognize as Mary. Behind me I heard Olive gasp.

"He threw me away," Melanie shouted. "So I killed that cow who stole him from me, took the ring that should have been mine, and buried her with him. He wanted her more than me? Fine. He could have her dead body on top of him for all eternity then."

A picture dropped off the wall, landing with a crash on the floor. Melanie jumped and spun around, her eyes wide. A decorative candle holder flew off the shelf and hit the woman in the arm, followed by a stapler from the desk and a vase with a fake spray of daisies in it.

"Stop," Melanie shrieked, covering her eyes.

"You shot me," Olive snarled in a voice that wasn't her own. "You drove David to his death with your crazy stalking and you shot me. I'll make sure you never have a moment's peace in your life for that, make sure you rot in hell after you're dead."

Suddenly the room was filled with flying objects. I ducked down to the floor while Melanie tried to bat them away, finally turning and fleeing the room.

Olive collapsed to the floor and I hesitated, unsure whether to go to my friend or chase after Melanie.

"Go," Suzette shouted as she sprang forward to help Olive.

She didn't have to tell me twice. I took off and exited the

building in time to see Melanie peel away in her car, speeding far above the ten mile per hour limit of the cemetery roads. I got in my car as well, but she'd gotten a head start on me and I wasn't exactly a race car driver.

Luckily, neither was Melanie. Her little Kia weaved around the turns, cutting into the grass and at one point even smashing the bumper against a grave marker. I sped up as I saw her heading for the entrance, wondering if the police would be able to put an APB out on her and catch her before she managed to ditch the car and flee the country. Just as she neared the gate, I saw an SUV block the entrance. Melanie slammed on her breaks, the Kia fishtailing to the side and smashing head-on into the iron fence.

A man in an ill-fitting navy suit got out of the SUV, gun drawn as he demanded that Melanie step out of the car. I swear I'd never seen Miles look so darned sexy. If Violet were here now, she definitely would have said "yes" to a date with this man.

Two sheriff's vehicles pulled up behind the SUV. As men poured from them, I recognized Detective Norris. I eased my sedan over to the side of the road and saw Miles pull Melanie from the Kia and cuff her as he recited her Miranda rights.

Yep, totally sexy. Not quite as sexy as Judge Beck in his courtroom with his robes and his stern gaze, but still sexy.

With a smile, I turned my car around and headed back to the cemetery office for Olive and Suzette. We'd give our statements to the police about the confession and the letters later. Right now, we had the last bit of a graveside service to attend, and afterward we'd head over to the church for some chicken salad sandwiches, punch, and a celebration of Ford Branch's life.

And maybe there in the church, Sarah and DeLanie would be able to finally put the past behind them and forgive.

CHAPTER 22

"So…. how was the vacation?" I asked Daisy as I contorted myself into Kapotasana. My lackadaisical yoga practice the past week was making itself evident in my stiff muscles and the pigeon pose ended up looking more like a deflated backward triangle.

"It was good." She smirked.

"So I take it the sheets weren't even creased in that second bedroom?" I huffed, wondering how Daisy could manage this pose so effortlessly. Had she been doing her yoga while in the Keys with J.T.? Or maybe their sex had involved some kinky contorted positions that were clearly beyond my abilities.

"I slept in my own bedroom." She chuckled. "We got pretty hot and heavy, but I wanted to wait. Let's just say that J.T. took more cold showers in the last week then he probably has in his whole lifetime."

We rose, Daisy with graceful core muscle control, and me nearly toppling on the grass. Then we moved into the much more comfortable Child's Pose.

"Great. Is there a date you have in mind to actually do the

deed with the poor man, or do you intend to lead him on indefinitely?" I asked.

"I'm making him dinner next week and plan on having dessert go on until the morning. Don't tell him, though. It's a surprise."

As if I would tell my boss that sort of thing.

"I hear *you* had an exciting week," she commented as we moved into a plank position, then Uttanasana. "Catching a murderer and all that."

Detective Norris had been much quicker than I'd thought about checking the pawn shop records. Somehow that had been enough for him to get a warrant, so while we were all at a funeral, the detective and other deputies were busy searching Melanie's house. There they found the gun—the same caliber that was used to shoot Mary. They also found lots of pictures of David. That along with the letters we'd found in Melanie's office, plus her confession to Olive, Suzette, and me were more than enough for them to get a conviction. The woman was going to jail.

And I hadn't seen Mary's ghost since. I hoped the woman was finally at rest. I hoped both she and David were finding peace together in eternity.

"Yes, I caught a murderer. Although I had some help from a detective and from Olive."

We moved into Warrior Pose. "You'll need to tell J.T. all about it when you get in," Daisy said. "Don't say I told you, but he was worried sick about his business the whole time we were in the Keys. I get the idea that man doesn't take many vacations. I'll give him credit though, he trusted you enough to not call and check up on you even once while we were gone."

"Good. Although he'll have to wait for my updates because I'm going in late today. I've got to be here for the dishwasher installation."

"You finally got a new dishwasher!" Daisy exclaimed. "Tell me about it. Has it got all the features you wanted? Does it match your cabinetry? I'm so glad you were able to buy a new one."

I smiled serenely as we moved to a tree pose. "It's a basic dishwasher. It's reliable and has a warranty through the appliance store. It's white with a little dent on one side and a tiny bit of rust on the bottom. And I got a very good deal on it."

I did. There was a bit of money left in my savings account and I'd add to that each paycheck to build up my safety net once more. I'd realized that having that cushion of savings was far more important to me than fancy features on a dishwasher or avoiding any embarrassment over my ability to afford fancy, expensive appliances. It cleaned the dishes. It was reliable and functional. And at the end of the day, that's what mattered the most.

"Sounds a whole lot better than doing dishes by hand," Daisy said, absolutely confirming that I'd made the right choice.

"It is. And it's a lot better than having to rewash dishes because the kids missed a spot and there's old coffee around the rim of my mug."

Daisy laughed, and the sound was so infectious that I laughed as well.

"It's good to have you back," I told my best friend as we finished up our yoga.

"It's good to be back." She gave me a big hug and we went inside to enjoy apple spice muffins and coffee, and to wait for the dishwasher installation.

ACKNOWLEDGMENTS

Special thanks to Lyndsey Lewellen for cover design and typography, and to both Erin Zarro and Kimberly Cannon for copyediting.

ABOUT THE AUTHOR

Libby Howard lives in a little house in the woods with her sons and two exuberant bloodhounds. She occasionally knits, occasionally bakes, and occasionally manages to do a load of laundry. Most of her writing is done in a bar where she can combine work with people-watching, a decent micro-brew, and a plate of Old Bay wings.

For more information:
libbyhowardbooks.com/

f

ALSO BY LIBBY HOWARD

<u>Locust Point Mystery Series:</u>

The Tell All

Junkyard Man

Antique Secrets

Hometown Hero

A Literary Scandal

Root of All Evil

A Grave Situation

Last Supper (February 2019)